Mama's Little Bones

and

Other Stories

Mama's Little Bones

and

Other Stories

*For Frances and David,
two dear friends...!*

By

[signature]

Rita Sturam Wirkala

All Bilingual Press
www.allbilingual.com

ISBN: 978-1-7368488-7-6

Printed in the U.S.A.

Other books by the author

Novels

El Encuentro - Ed. Pearson, Madrid, 2011

The Encounter - ABP, Seattle, 2014

Las aguas del Kalahari - ABP, Seattle, 2018

YA novels

Tarsiana - ABP (Bilingüe español-inglés), 2011

Tales for The Dreamer - Hoopoe Books, 2018

Cuentos para El Soñador - ABP, Seattle, 2019

Short Stories

Los huesitos de mamá y otros relatos - Ed. Laborde, Argentina, 2018

Años bisiestos: Cinco historias argentinas- ABP, Seattle, 2021

Children's Poetry

Mis primeros poemas - ABP, 2014

Poemas para chicos y grandes - ABP, Vol. 1, 2013

Poemas para chicos y grandes - ABP, Vol. 2, 2015

Essays

La Magia de la palabra. Guía para la escritura creativa en español - ABP, 2020

Huellas del Sufismo en el "Libro de Buen amor del Arcipreste de Hita" (Doctoral dissertation) - ABP, 2021

Spanish Language curriculum

Español para los chiquitos, Text, Audiobook, Activity book and Parent-Teacher Guide - ABP, 2006

Español para chicos y grandes, Level 1. **John Hopkins University CTY curriculum.** Text, Manual and Audio book - ABP, 2004, 2011, 2018

Español para chicos y grandes, Level 2. **John Hopkins University CTY curriculum.** Text, Manual and Audio book - ABP, 2009, 2016

Los viajes de Rosa y Ernesto- A Step by Step Spanish Reader. Book 1. Text, Manual and Audio book - ABP, 2009, 2007

Los viajes de Rosa y Ernesto- A Step by Step Spanish Reader. Book 2. Text, Manual and Audio book - ABP, 2013

Bobi y Cuqui en español: Chistes y aventuras del dúo canino. (Comics with English translations) - ABP 2021

To the memory of my grandfather,
co-founder of our town, *María Susana*.

CONTENTS

PROLOGUE by JOYCE YARROW

What a treat to read stories that not only transport you to another place and time but welcome you to stay there.

The author uses twists of irony, humor and snippets of philosophy to augment the suspense and unpredictability of these lively and loosely autobiographical tales, set in her Argentinian hometown of María Susana. The triangular shaped town is populated by a wonderful cross section of humanity, a place where thieves work feverishly behind the scenes on Tango night, Tonino the village Fool unwittingly predicts a supposedly winning lottery number, and the ghost of a suicide is blamed for everything from losing an earring to burning a stew.

Rita Wirkala switches between microcosm and macrocosm effortlessly. In *Amelia and I*, she confesses her sin of bullying her friend who came from the "Other Side" of the railroad tracks that divide the town. As a small child, she absorbed the prejudices around her, and as her "mature self" she asks the hard questions: "What instincts are stirred when an affectionate and docile dog suddenly jumps at a beggar or drunkard and establishes his bestial supremacy? What ancient substrates of our psyches surface when the stimulus—just as archaic—brushes a nerve in the center of power and hierarchy, and the mechanism of evil is reestablished?" She is eventually reunited with Amelia, and I don't know what moved me more— the author's acceptance of her own culpability or Amelia's instinctive willingness to forgive.

Each story is firmly rooted in small town life while at the same time being an integral piece of a larger picture. In *Dissonances I,* the author has her first experience of guilt after watching an erotic peep show at the amusement park. We follow her journey from finding comfort in prayer to becoming disillusioned with the village priest and dropping the dogma of the church "like the butterfly leaves the chrysalis that no longer serves as its support." How extraordinary that, at the age of eleven, she finds her own way of defining Divinity.

In *Mama's Little Bones,* the Delfino sisters serve Pernod to visiting children in elegant cordial glasses and, after cleaning their dead mother's bones in the family pantheon, have an explosive falling out over a missing wedding ring. When I came to the line, "Outside the rain fell like a round of applause," the description fit their theatrics so well that I laughed aloud.

Although taking place in the past, these stories come from a deep source that has continued to nourish the author's writing. It is as if her childhood experiences have blossomed in her adult life, so that each story is a flower, the petals colored by her independent thinking, psychological insight, and entertaining humor.

— June 2, 2022

Joyce Yarrow. Author of *Zahara and the Lost Books of Light, Sandstorm* and several mystery novels.

PROLOGUE by the author

Among the recent comments I have received from my former townspeople in Argentina, one stands out for its ironic truth:

"To think that we all wanted to leave the town and now we all want to go back!"

I was one of those who left, at the age of twelve. And unlike Antonio Machado's traveler, I have never looked back. I cut the ties with my eyes closed, with a single chop of the knife. Today I regret it.

When we go down the *final stretch*—to use an expression popular with the horseracing lovers of the Argentine pampas—we tend to evoke the *initial* stretch, our most distant past, as well. Still, memory is an impressionistic landscape that only suggests contours. At other times, our reflections suggest a cubist painting in which one recomposes the images at will.

The distance that separates me from the world of my childhood, doubly vast in its temporal and geographical dimensions, at first made it difficult for me to recover experiences and put them into writing. However, after many days spent waiting at the door to the layer of consciousness where our memories are hidden, they have begun to take shape. I also owe a debt to my friends—those who have maintained a closer link with the place and those who still live there—whose shared recollections have made it possible for me to compose these chronicles and stories.

Writing a memoir is an attempt to lengthen life. One appears in the world, shines a bit like a shooting star, and then vanishes into the twilight. Hence our eagerness to leave a mark. Yet most marks are as evanescent as footprints in the sand: the tide comes in and erases our tracks.

The idea of disappearing altogether—at least in the form of the "I" we know—makes some of us humbler and terrifies others. (The similar sound of "terrified" and "terra" is no accident: both words come from the same terrifying root). For me, the approach of sunset is not an affliction. Instead, it impels me to write, and in this I delight. Consequently, these stories are not loaded with nostalgia, but rather with the joy of being able to celebrate some lives and rekindle seminal events.

As in any book based on early memories rather than written chronicles, some segments are all true, and others nuanced with a good dose of imagination.

There is *what was, what perhaps was,* and *what could have been.*

Some are intimate remembrances of my own and others have been gleaned from the experiences of my friends, but they all revolve around this triangular town sketched like a life-size drawing on the fertile lands of the Argentine pampas.

These stories can be read linearly or randomly, from the middle, forward, or back—or in any order and disorder. Because that is how they inhabit my own memory.

In some cases, I have not changed the names of the people who appear in my tales. In other instances, I modified them slightly, to respect their privacy (*on earth as it is in heaven*). Therefore, any suspicious similarity to real names is not by mistake.

Mama's Little Bones

The flavor of anise always reminds me of the Delfino sisters. They used to serve my cousin and me Pernod in elegant little cordial glasses every time we visited when we were kids.

The sisters lived at the village edge where the wheat fields and pastures began. This was decades ago, long before wheat, sunflower, flax and corn yielded to the now-ubiquitous soybeans, and before ranchers started sending their cattle to be fattened in feedlots.

We called them Aunt Serafina, or Auntie Fina, and Aunt Immacolata, or Auntie Ima. They were my cousin Alicia's aunts, not mine, but since I was Alicia's cousin, we were both free to wander into their patio without knocking. We would sometimes stop there to use the bathroom while we were running around the neighborhood. In that house it was a privy off the patio—nothing more than a hole over a little platform, which the ladies called the "sanitary."

On those occasions they would invite us into the parlor and show us the many family photographs hanging on the walls. Sometimes they would bring out an old shotgun they referred to as a "9-millimeter." This seemed to us rather absurd since it was clearly much longer than that. Somehow, they must have thought that seeing it would be an edifying experience for us girls who would one day be women.

Then they would open the crystal hutch and the bottle would appear along with the little cordial glasses. We would take slow sips as if it were the elixir of the gods. Auntie Ima was the more generous of the two and always offered a second round. Serafina, the elder, had taken it upon herself to manage the household expenses and was therefore more parsimonious. Her excuse was that, since we were only 10, the alcohol might go to our heads.

It did happen sometimes, but not often.

The principal attraction was not the photos or the liqueur, which burned our throats, but the ombú standing in the middle of the patio. That huge Pampas tree, which isn't really even a tree but a giant tree-like grass, was where my cousin and I would commune with the natural world, curling up in the hollows of its voluptuous roots.

The Delfino sisters, by contrast, were not generously proportioned like the ombú, but very thin and as tall as cypresses, those cemetery trees that are impossible to climb. People used to refer to them disparagingly as "dry" or as "dry as salt cod".

The sisters' main virtue was their cleanliness. Both dressed in black. Not because they were widows, since neither had enjoyed the pleasures of married life or, as they put it, suffered the unpleasantness of men, those coarse, filthy beings. They started wearing black when their mother died and hadn't stopped since. They wore black skirts, black embroidered blouses, black winter stockings, and black shawls every day to morning mass. Just as black were their hair, their eyes and their thick Sicilian eyebrows.

Once a month the sisters would climb into their Model T Ford—which was black as well and a relic even then—and drive the kilometer and a half to the cemetery with the wholesome purpose of cleaning the family pantheon. When their mother died, the family had buried her in a cheap pine coffin in the ground. At the time, even though their father had inherited a bit of land, they were not by any stretch well off. By the end of the 40s, however, when landholders had made fortunes exporting meat and wheat to European countries at war, Mr. Delfino had felt more prosperous. He no longer had to toil, stooped and sweating, in the fields like before. He was able, even, to buy a thresher and a harvester and grow a hefty bank account. Conscious of his own mortality, he built a mausoleum, known as a "pantheon" in those parts, in the town cemetery, as did all the upper-middle-class families, where family members were laid to rest. As is well known, bodies laid to rest in this manner do not decompose as quickly as those in coffins placed in common tombs. Nor did they fraternize with the more plebeian skeletons of just any old neighbor in the earthen graves.

When the construction was complete, Doña Delfino's remains, which were by now loose bones, were placed with proper ceremony in an urn gracing the pantheon's small altar. Don Delfino died some years later and took his position in a luxurious casket against the left-hand wall. Places were reserved for the sisters when their hour arrived, on cement platforms to the right, one above the other, like bunkbeds.

This stark white pantheon was not as grand as others, but it had an imposing set of carved wooden doors, opulently decorated with angels. The sisters' monthly visit followed an established routine. As soon as they entered, they would open the small round clerestory window and brush the spiderwebs off the cherubim and other plaster ornaments. After cleaning the floor, the sisters would apply their feather dusters to their father's coffin, by now dusty from all the sweeping. They would then give the silver candelabra, as well as the altar with its various saints from the abundant Catholic Olympus, a good shine. Finally, they would clean their mother's urn, a type of large jar with a lid. This always gave them some trouble. The material, not particularly fine, resisted both water and sponge. The humidity of the place caused a light white film, akin to some type of mold, to form just minutes after cleaning, and it would surface again and again as if bewitched.

On one of their visits, after cleaning, lighting the candles and saying the rosary, the sisters agreed to give up pointlessly scrubbing of the urn and buy another of finer material.

"Carrara marble," Ima proposed.

"It's so expensive," her sister objected. "Let's go for Chinese marble—it's good quality but cheaper."

And, because Fina signed the checks and so had the upper hand, Chinese marble it was.

By that time, my father had closed his shop, which was selling next to nothing, and had taken a job as sales representative for a mortuary house. His catalog pictured gravestones, caskets and urns for niches or tombs, of bronze or marble, some with a small built-in vessel where water and flowers could be placed. Epitaphs were included in the price. Mourners could either specify the wording themselves or accept one of the salesperson's suggestions. I loved to come up with phrases for my father to use during his sales, such as "Living in our hearts," "Resting in the arms of Jesus," and "At peace with the Lord."

I am proud to say that these were my first published works.

But back to the catalog, which also contained images of beautiful chests and amphorae in various materials where ashes or bones could be stored. The

Delfinos wanted the best urn available—or almost the best—and this was good news for my father, who earned a commission on his sales. I remember the day they chose one from the display, and also the day that the distributor, a man we called *"comisionista,"* brought it from the city. Ima had placed the order, because the man had a grudge against her sister. He said Fina was stingy and distrustful.

The day after the urn arrived, the sisters got into their Model T and went straight to the cemetery. Ima drove, as always, and Serafina said the rosary while muttering about how much their bank account had gone down after the extravagant, though necessary, expense. The ability to compartmentalize was one of her talents. Because it was a weekday, the sisters found the cemetery empty. They were pleased about this, since they did not appreciate curious onlookers. I know this and other details because my cousin told me, and she heard it from her mother, who heard it from Serafina herself during her sister Immacolata's wake.

Serafina said they parked the Model T under a weeping willow near the cemetery wall, opened the wrought-iron gates and made their way down the alley leading to the family pantheon. The urn must have been very heavy, but the sisters, though skinny, were not weak. They had spunk, as they say, and determination. I can imagine them walking and sweating in their long black dresses as they passed the silver crosses and the white tombs, carrying the marble jar between them for over 200 meters. I know the place well, and I know where the Delfinos are because on the Day of the Dead, when the villagers went to pray and place fresh flowers on graves, my friends and I would play hide and seek among the tombs and pantheons.

That day, when Ima opened the pantheon door, the hinges gave out an alarming shriek, which her sister felt was a bad omen. Serafina lit the lantern and pulled the chord that opened the clerestory windows. Brilliant light filled the mausoleum. She found matches and lit six candles, which produced a strange luminosity in combination with the natural light.

They set to work. After crossing themselves several times, Ima gently shook the old urn: a dry clatter told her the bones had not yet been reduced to dust. Good! Removing the cover, she began to take out, one by one, the bony remains of her late mother, laying them in a neat row on the altar.

At this point I must pause in my narrative so as not to be accused of telling tall tales. It's true that Serafina did not specify whether she had or hadn't seen the ring shining among the bones at that moment, and for this reason I cannot affirm that she had. She only mentioned that after a few minutes her sister Ima began to sneeze. An insidious dust filled her nostrils.

"This is disgusting, Fina," Ima commented. "We have to wash them."

Her sister agreed. There was no other way. The bones were pocked and pitted and covered with a dry residue. It would be undignified to ignore this fact. Always diligent and hard-working—no one could deny her these virtues—Serafina went looking for the bucket of water that cemeteries always have for filling vases, and also a towel they had in the Model T. When she returned to the pantheon, she saw that Ima had moved the bones onto a cloth on the floor. They got ready to clean them one by one.

"And didn't you feel ... how should I put it ... strange, doing this?" Alicia's mom asked when she heard the story from Serafina later.

"No, no... After all, it's one's mother, not just

any old skeleton," Fina assured her. "And of course, dear, dust to dust, you know. But I must say those bones were in awful shape. And I told my sister, Ima, for the love of God, we have to do a good job.'"

And so began the meticulous cleaning operation. Ima handed the bones over to Fina one at a time, and Fina submerged them in the bucket before giving them a stir and returning them to her sister, who dried them with the towel and carefully placed them in the new urn. In the gloomy silence not even the slightest click could be heard as Ima was very careful when it came to handling, with her delicate bird-like fingers each and every bone and arranging them in the brand new urn. The little bones of the hands and feet gave them the most trouble. "There were so many!" Fina remarked. Every now and again they had to change the water, which would quickly become murky. An hour later, when they had finished up the task and were sitting on the ground for a well-deserved rest, an image crossed Fina's mind.

"Wasn't mama buried with her wedding ring, Ima?"

"I don't know, Fina, but we would have seen it, don't you think?"

"I suppose so…"

So the sisters' macabre task ended. And, for the record, "macabre" is my addition; to them, it was just a sacred duty to filial love and cleanliness.

Some days later, with Ima absent, Serafina took the family photo album from a closet. There she found a photograph of her mother in her casket, in a lacy dress and a with bouquet of silken flowers. And she confirmed what was already circulating in the silent labyrinth of her memory: the gold ring with its little diamonds clearly sparkled on her mother's ring finger. She consulted with the mortician, Mr. Di Celio. He told her he had personally supervised the transfer of her mother's mortal remains from the original coffin, and that the ring was still on the corresponding metacarpal of her left hand, though a little looser, of course, when they sealed the urn. His probity was beyond doubt. Di Celio was a man of the church, her father's countryman, an all-around honorable man, and also rich. Certainly not a petty thief. Besides, there were witnesses. No, it couldn't have been him or any of his employees. There was only one abominable answer to the puzzle: Ima had been alone with the bones of their progenitor when Fina had gone for water. She had had sufficient time to ... ah, the thought was so ugly it made her skin crawl. She rejected it the instant it flowered in her mind. And yet, it began to obsess her relentlessly.

From that day forward, Serafina watched her sister very carefully. She noticed that Ima was praying more than usual and that the contents of the Pernod bottle went down according to the frequency of her devotions. Not only that, but on two occasions that week Ima disappeared toward the end of the afternoon and returned after nightfall, with the excuse of having been distributing stamps of the Virgin and other pious explanations that didn't quite ring true. All this was accompanied by a new light in Ima's eyes, rosier cheeks and shinier lips, in contrast to her usual pallor. Fina decided to follow her.

It must have been July or August, because the weather was cold. She put on a pair of mechanic's overalls, one of her late father's jackets and a hat. Fina mounted her bicycle and glided through the shadows of a winter's evening, taking care to avoid the streetlights' dim glow. It is not easy to go about incognito in a village. When the streets are deserted, there are spies peering through shutters with curious eyes. And the gossipers are plenty. One of these was old Fiorella. The sisters knew her well. Once, when she had fallen drunk into a ditch full of water and frogs, the two had rescued her, taken her home, bathed her and left her cleanly sleeping it off in bed. It had been an act of Christian charity.

Immacolata, as it turned out, was going to the old harpy's house without telling her sister!

Fina stationed herself in shadows and took up her vigil. Consumed by anxiety, she waited and waited. Thank God she had her rosary to occupy the long minutes as well as her lips. It was at least 8 o'clock when the front door opened and out walked her sister. Something told her to stay put and continue watching that portent-laden door. After a few minutes, a male figure emerged, not by the front door but from the back. It was the *comisionista.*

Adrenaline ran riot through Serafina's veins, and her mind raced frantically as she imagined various reasons for this obviously secret encounter. She considered the possibilities. There were only two explanations, each one worse than the other. The first was that Ima was negotiating with the *comisionista* and trying to get the best price for the ring. This was unsatisfactory. Why would her sister need money? True, Fina, in her strict administrative function, was a little stingy—as was her duty. But...Ima did not lack for anything! The other option was that the pair... a flurry of obscene scenarios assailed her. She was furious. Unthinkable! Just the thought was so overwhelming she felt nauseated. Ranting, she flew back home, pedaling furiously so as to get there before her sister She ran to her room, changed clothes and came out holding a handkerchief to her mouth and a faking a coughing fit to hide her fury. She began to cook dinner.

That night the elder sister was able, through great effort, to stifle the volcano inside her. They ate in silence—a thick, electric silence. Without proof, Fina could not blame her sister for anything. Nor could she muster the strength to ask her sister straight out about her rendezvous. She did not wish to be accused by Ima of tawdry espionage. No, she needed to act calmly and with intelligence. Her sense of premonition, which often flared like a beacon in a fog when she imagined catastrophes, now led her to immediate action. As soon as her sister began to snore, Serafina put on a woolen smock that for some time now had showed its age, got the flashlight and, in the grip of fierce determination, went out to the garbage can on the sidewalk. It had been there all week. The garbageman would be by tomorrow. She brought the garbage can inside, hid it behind the ombú against the remote chance that Ima might open the window, and began to pick through the garbage—discarded Yerba Mate leaves, potato peels, eggshells, chicken bones and other leftovers—what little the spartan Delfino sisters tossed into the garbage. It was not difficult to find what she was looking for, because it was the only thing wrapped in newspaper: the incriminating cloth.

¡Ave María Purísima! There could be no doubt! Her sister's panties stained with blood! And it wasn't menstrual blood, because their periods were nowhere near due, she knew, because in this they were quite synchronized.

Ima had lost her virginity!

Serafina uttered an enraged prayer, put her sister's rag in the woolen smock's pocket and went back into the house. She did not sleep a wink that night. Mentally, she reviewed the seven cardinal sins, and then the venal ones. Robbery was cardinal. So was lying...but disloyalty? Why did it not figure among the cardinal sins? Had Moses run out of space on his stone tablets?

She got up weary-eyed, her face ashen, her breath foul, and could not stop herself from confronting Ima, who was preparing mate.

"I don't know which is worse, stealing or lying!" she spat, with fiery eyes and a demented look, holding the incriminating undergarment aloft.

Ima froze and went white as a ghost.

"You lied, you robbed, you FORNICATED! That will get you sent to hell three times over, sister!" Fina continued. "Out with it, what did you do with Mama's ring? Did you give it as a present to your Mr. So-and-so, to pay for his services, maybe?"

Ima did not answer. She locked herself in her room and did not come out for a long time. Well, she did come out at one point, like a thundercloud—Fina corrected herself when she told the story—just to get the anis from the crystal cabinet—and then locked herself in once more. After several hours, by which time Fina's knuckles hurt from knocking on the door, her sister finally came out, quite drunk, and said:

"You want to know where the ring is, yes sister?

Come, I'll show you!"

She stumbled over the patio in the direction of the privy, opened the door, drew the ring from her pocket and said to her sister:

"There's your ring, go ahead and get it!" And she let it fall into the stinking hole.

The days following this event were a little confused in Serafina's telling. It seems that the sisters did not speak to each other ever again. And it seems that Ima only left her room to go to the parlor like a whipped dog for a swig from the bottle. Then she would go back into her room and lock the door. In a couple of days, she had downed a second bottle, 35% proof, they say, even though Fina was sure that it had been more. And when she finished, she put it on the dresser with a candle stuck into it.

What was indeed clear was that, on the third day, a rainy one, Ima packed up her things and disappeared, leaving only the following message:

Envy is also a cardinal sin. See you in Hell, sister! The ring was for a white dress. No matter. I'll get married in black.

Outside, the rain fell like a round of applause.

Fina held a symbolic funeral because, she said,

her sister was dead to her.

As for the unfortunate ring, they say she got a lantern and, with a hook at the end of a stick, fished it out with no trouble at all. It was still intact shining atop of the pile of excrement.

"I sold the ring to my neighbor," Fina said, "but the money wasn't enough for the funeral, even though there was no body.

"And didn't you feel it was … disgusting, fishing around in the privy?" asked my aunt.

"No, no. It was our shit, after all, not just anyone's shit."

Amelia and I

Before filing into the classroom, we would form a line by order of height. Since she was a bit shorter, Amelia was always right in front of me. Day after day I pinched her neck, and she never made a sound. My mother was the school's music teacher. That's why, by the age of six, I already had my privileges. Amelia had no mother. What she had was humility.

The memory of my guilt lay dormant in some hidden zone deep inside for five decades, until one day it surfaced when I received an email. Someone had found me on this stage we call Facebook, this vast virtual habitat we use to show off, to praise or insult each other across the globe. Sometimes, though, it allows us to discover, in some twisted digital hallway or other, a friend from the past with whom we have lost touch. In my case, this friend ended up connecting me with Amelia, fifty years after I left my village. Amelia, my friend from the Other Side.

What you need to know is that our town was actually two towns divided by railroad tracks. Over here, the Italian settlers who came to Argentina at the beginning of the twentieth century—we called them *gringos*—and other Europeans. Over there, the *criollos*[1], the long-suffering mestizos who had lived in these lands since colonial times. On one side, the prosperous white people; on the other, the poor, the *morochos*, the *negros*. On one side, my family; on the other, Amelia's.

Let's not forget: when the Americas were terra incognita, in this part of the continent roamed the Tehuelches, the Ranqueles, the Puelches, the Picunches, and the other aboriginal peoples of the pampas. As in all Latin America, the conquerors mated, by hook or by crook, with the native women. They gave them children and even Spanish surnames, but not the inheritances they reserved for their "legitimate" descendants.

---

[1] *Criollo* in Argentina is the mixed race of Spaniard and indigenous.

Following the Conquest came olive-skinned Spanish *moriscos* who had long lost their Arabic language and their Islamic religion, but not their love of the guitar and of poetry, of horses and of daggers. The union of Spaniard—white or morisco—and Indian, together with minstrelsy and knife fights and love affairs, also gave birth to those landless and lawless nomads of the pampas called gauchos.

The gaucho lifestyle declined as progress and mass immigration from Europe got underway, but despite many efforts they could not be evicted. Degraded and marginalized, most of them became poor peons, without the benefit of either collective memory or prospects, living on brutal land that didn't belong to them. They became stoic via force and abuse.

The land was sold at public auction to English investors and later to other Europeans, and by the end of the 20th century was entirely fenced off. The mestizos, for social, financial, or historical reasons, were not invited.

This is a story repeated around the country, multiplied in the mirrors of time; and in this way my town is no different from others. What is unique is its geography.

The land's new owner, in his eagerness to attract a railway station to his domain, surrendered an area of triangular shape—I suspect that a square would have been too lavish—to found the colony, which took the name of the donor's daughter: María Susana. The area was split in two by the train tracks, creating a small triangle and a trapezoid, and the town's civic center located on the latter. As was customary, María Susana was configured around a square plaza, with its flagpole and flag, its swings and other playground equipment, a few trees, and a profusion of ornamental plants.

Everything seemed well planned, until the torrential rains came: this town was not only triangulated; it was built on an incline too. When folks realized that they had established the town center in the lower portion, where rainwater from the entire region flooded the plain and formed immense lagoons, they began to favor the upper part, on the opposite side of the railroad. This was where the more prosperous immigrants settled. Among these settlers was my grandfather, hailing from the Italian shores of the Adriatic, who established a beverage business even before the streets were opened on the town's upper side.

It was the year 1910.

Soon, houses with European facades were built, businesses were erected, vaulted streets with ditches on both sides were opened, and the church and school were founded.

The impoverished mestizos remained on the lower side, where their houses of bare bricks and huts of pure adobe sprouted.

This is how the division was gradually created, separating the settlers of María Susana according to skin and surname.

The railroad tracks were barely four inches of steel rising out of a rich and wide land. Such a small thing! And yet... My grandparents and other colonists called those habitants from the *barrio* "los negros" and tolerated them—so long as they stayed on the Other Side.

It is true that on Christmas night, when we had already distributed the gifts and extinguished the small candles that lit our trees with their trembling flames, groups of young people from the other side of town would come with their guitars to serenade under our windows, waiting for the traditional reward: a bottle of wine. Also, on San Roque's Day, they would cross over to take part in the festivities in honor of the town's patron saint. They would get up on the dance hall stage and bellow epic, octosyllabic gaucho verses full of nostalgia and courage. For the rest of the year they remained, tacitly ostracized, on the Other Side. At night we could hear only the toads croaking from the ponds when the barrio was flooded out.

Amelia lived over there with her father, her siblings, their croaking toads, and their poverty.

Crossing over was said to be dangerous during the day, when the train barreled through our town, blindly and implacably, with utter disrespect for class and race. At night, *La Llorona* was equally menacing, as she wailed her plaintive song of Medea, bent on washing her guilt away with human blood. Children's blood especially.

The agricultural cooperative was in our part of town and customers came from afar to tie their horses to the *palenque* out front, a steel bar going from tree to tree. While the owners were buying things for their fields, the horses spread dung cakes near the gutter. But neither the dung nor the effluvia of urine that rose to our noses prevented us kids from swinging on the *palenque* and soaring over the top of the fresh manure crowned with flies. After all, the plaza with the play-ground, a remnant of an urban planning error, had remained on the Other Side of the tracks that could not be crossed.

Sometimes, Amelia's father would visit the co-operative on his horse to buy some food for his pigs or, most probably, his employer's pigs. He may have been a peon from some ranch, I don't know. What I do know is that he was a gaucho all right: boots and spurs, baggy pants, coins on his belt, poncho, and a bandanna around his neck. And he played the guitar. His name was Páez, *morisco*[2] surname.

In contrast, my father was a merchant who, and on both sides, was a descendant of those from northern Italy with a good portion of Germanic blood flowing through their veins. My mother? Pure Roman.

For some reason—perhaps the music classes— Amelia's father wanted her to attend our school and not the smaller one on the Other Side. That is why, every day, Amelia crossed over, fearless. She crossed over the plaza, the vacant lots, the wilderness where La Llorona lived, the tracks and through the train

---

[2] A Spaniard Moorish converted to Christianity.

station, rain or shine, to go to the school for the well-off. And I, a well-brought-up little girl from a good family, would pinch her neck as we stood in line listening to the chords of our national anthem.

We grew up, and with the year of pinching behind us, Amelia and I became friends. Sadly, I never ventured over to the Other Side. And then, one splendorous summer day she invited me over. I went with some other girls from my side of town. We saw her house, but only from the outside—a little box of raw brick, with its old well and bucket, and the adobe bread oven set on a patio of beaten earth. Amelia showed us around the neighborhood. There were no elaborate bars on the windows or ornate cornices on the ceilings, like ours. Some houses were similar to hers, others humbler still. It seemed to me they had been made of the same elemental substance, with the patience and tenderness of the *horneros*, those birds of the pampas that build their nests of mud and straw, brown and round, stuck to the tops of fence posts. There was something healthy and wild in all that, a beautiful and simple air that gave us pleasure.

On we walked in our patent leather shoes and white stockings, our feet sinking into the mud, until we came to the pond. We threw rocks at the toads, especially the ones that happened to be mating.

What had been for me, until that day, just a mental abstraction—the Other Side—suddenly became concrete reality on a bright summer day.

Amelia bridged the two sides of my divided village and guided me to that Other World I had ignored.

Fifty years later we met again in the village. We hugged, we cried. I asked her, in a moment of courage, if she remembered my torturing her. Yes, she remembered it. She also shrugged it off.

"How could you have forgiven me?" I insisted.

"You were only six years old! Why wouldn't I? It was just jealousy."

True enough, my mother would come to teach her music class every day, bringing lunch for me and another one for the little motherless Páez girl. And every day Amelia would return to her house on the other side of the tracks with her stomach full and her neck bruised.

I want to believe that it was jealousy. I tremble to think I punished her for being an orphan, for being different, for being a toad from another pond. Or maybe just for being docile. I'm thinking of the human brain divided into two hemispheres: one, dominant, with the arrogance of noisy logic; the other silent, with the light subtlety of intuitive thought. But what is it that divides a little girl's heart down the middle, separating its sweet and its perverse sides? What instincts are stirred when an affectionate and docile dog suddenly jumps at a beggar or drunkard and establishes his bestial supremacy? What ancient substrates of our psyches surface when the stimulus—just as archaic—brushes a nerve in the center of power and hierarchy, and the mechanism of evil is reestablished? *Let's build a wall because they are not ours! Let us pour our anger on them because they are different! Let's pinch their children's necks! because they are poor, because they are outsiders. Do not trespass, do not cross to this side of the tracks! Get out!*

The mind is a world in miniature, just a fractal of human society, in which the Other is detested and must be crushed. My childish self would have responded with arcane force to those unwritten rules of racism and tribalism.

Otherness is detestable.

I sit at my keyboard. It's the same whenever soul-searching forces a confession. This one clouds my vision, and my eyes tear up. I am overflowing with long-buried emotions fighting to get out, to burst out, from that fold of mind where my Contrite Self lives. I stroke a few keys, I lift my trembling hand, I feel for the glass of white wine beside me. My readers may say, "Such an outsized reproach for such a trifling sin!" But the big or the small may not matter: all must be weighed in the balance.

My current self looks back in horror at yesterday's self, frozen in memory, and wants to strangle her. Was it me, the same me? Or was it the nemesis of myself, coexisting within me? And yet, each stage of life is guided by a different identity, because consciousness—that fluid, mysterious phenomenon in constant process of change—is a product never completely finished. My mature self understands this and forgives me. Amelia has forgiven me as well.

I laugh at those who attribute their shady acts to the resentment of that wounded creature that they carry inside, to the bad example, the lack of examples, the social pressure, the moral confusion. "They taught me badly," they say, "they didn't teach me." Or they go with the satisfactory explanation of their Freudian analyst. And with that they are justified. How easy! More courage is required to admit that some spirits are made of noble material, backwards and forwards, while others show a smooth and refined weave on one side that turns over to reveal a rough and knotty mesh. And I was given this workmanship: an imprecise fabric with countless threads, with roughness, with some lines straight and neat, others crooked and clumsy; an ambiguous design that from time to time asks to be unwoven, corrected, and rewoven.

Amelia, on the other hand, received a more luminous material. I transcribe something she wrote to me in an email before our reunion:

I had two dolls in my life: one, made of cloth, that my mother bought me when I was four years old; and the other, the one that you gave me, that had a little crack in her head.

Cracked head? Reality turned into a metaphor, or the other way around? Could my gift have been a confused gesture, like "here you are, I broke her head, but she is yours, I am giving her to you?"

... and we played so much with her, with my sister Clara. I never forgot that doll, it was so cute! Nor do I forget how good you were to me, just like your mom.

Yes, there are souls that have nobler features than others, front and back.

I dry my cheeks, ashamed. I console myself that shame comes with a palliative and a saving grace. I think of the bridge Amelia extended between my world and hers, and the way I continued to cross it throughout the rest of my life, this viaduct that takes me to the Other Side. I look for it. I hold out a hand when I can, and I stop to listen to the toads singing in the Other Pond just across from my village.[3]

---

[3] A shorter version was published under the pseudonym of Gloria Storani en *Puentes* (Antología, *Seattle Escribe*, Seattle, U.S.A. 2017).

The cure

Dr. Posada had gone to the races in San Jorge. He didn't have to be at his office because it was Saturday. If someone became ill, they would call him over the radio: the telephone network would not reach town for another seven years. But no one would bother him because of a common stomachache like mine. What's more, it was fake.

It had been a week since I had received an invitation to the birthday party of a girl I barely knew, time enough for my uneasiness to build, because the invitation had not been extended to parents. We weren't friends, and I wasn't friends with her friends either, because we were not the same age. But since my family belonged to the community's so-called cultural elite (my mother was the music teacher), they were forced to include me on the list. There was another elite in the town, the agricultural one, made up of the few wealthy ranchers who had their modern houses in the urban center and a gang of peons with their foremen taking care of their hundreds of hectares of fields with their thousands of head of cattle. Surely their daughters would be among the guests. They were tall, pretty girls who knew how to ride, and greeted you with a kiss on both cheeks, not just on one like we did. They were well-bred people.

The dreaded day arrived, and hard reality reinforced and intensified my fear.

It wasn't because they dressed me in organdy, the loathsome, rough fabric that was worse than starch, because it didn't soften with handling or washing, and you had to put up with the exasperating scratchiness on your neck and armpits. Nor was it because of the stiff, shiny black patent leather shoes that completed my torment. All that was torture with a small "t". The other kind that mortified the soul rather than the flesh I wasn't expected: they sent me by myself.

Of course, I knew the way to her house by heart. I could have walked there with my eyes closed.

It was the same route I took almost every day to go to grandma's. Right for half a block, then diagonally left, two more blocks, and there it was. But that distance, for a shy six-year-old girl, could not be measured in blocks or meters but by degrees of distress. Primal fear of tangible danger is vastly different from the fear felt by the timid, who fear irrationally, but it's no less visceral for that. I would have preferred to go on my own to the other side of the train track and through the pine forest where La Llorona roamed at dusk. At least there I could run instead of having to face a crowd of human beings I didn't know.

My mother used to say she was also shy as a child. I must have inherited that piece of my temperament from her. But personal traits aren't discrete; you receive them as part of a genetic package of varied contents, which at times seem diabolically connected. And mine was bundled with a great sense of compliance when it came to my elders' expectations. Or was it cowardice? In short, I could not admit to feeling apprehensive. That's why I didn't say a word when they put a wrapped gift in my hands and sent me off, just like that.

I walked stoically through the shadowless

streets for two long blocks. The town was waking up little by little from its long siesta. The greengrocer, perched on the driver's seat of his cart, slowly passed by, advertising his produce through a cardboard bullhorn. Flies buzzed around the head of his Percheron, who was unable to swat them away with his tail. I kept on walking, clutching the gift under my arm as if my life depended on it. Joaquin the Mule, so called because of his disproportionate nose—and the only thing I remember about him—was coming from the opposite direction. I crossed to the other side of the street. Then I saw a boy with a sparrow in a wire cage. I looked away and crossed the street again. I continued on my way and, for the remaining two endless blocks, fed an anxiety that constricted my chest and made it hard for me to breathe.

I got to the house. I stood in front of the tall, carved, dark-wood door. Even standing on tiptoe with my arm outstretched, the brass ring was too high for me to reach. I would have to use my knuckles. I knocked softly, as though I were tapping on my own crystal heart. And I waited. Wasn't this the house? Yes, it was, because I could already hear the rattles and the sound of whistles and also those blowout whistles that curl out and in with a hateful atonal hiss, all mixed with the shouting coming from the party. I forced myself to knock on the door with more determination as I would for the rest of my life when finding myself before closed doors, not knowing if I would discover some gallows behind them. Nobody came. Except for Mr. Ripoll, the wine seller. He got out of his carriage, smiled at me, deposited a carafe of bubbling water, picked up the empty siphon and, still smiling kindly as he usually did, announced himself by imperiously knocking on the door using the brass ring, thus sealing my fate. Someone opened the door. It was the housemaid. She saw me, and picking up the soda siphon, said, "Come in." I looked at her and started to cry.

"What's going on, babe?" the girl asked.

"My stomach hurts!" I answered, not knowing which version of me let this out. And maybe it did hurt but I'm not sure. I only remember the painful knot tightening in my throat, my embarrassment, my failure over not being able to penetrate that thick, gray wall that separates a human being from the rest of humanity. the humanity that does not belong to her small clan.

The employee, who we would have called a "servant" in the days before we were conscious of political correctness, left the soda siphon in the hallway, yelled something into the interior of the house, took me by the hand and led me home. I cried all the way back. When we arrived, she explained to my mother that I was unwell, and left.

My mother was puzzled. My crying continued *in crescendo*, sometimes between hiccups and broken sobs, sometimes between howls and torrents of tears. It was a cry of rage at myself, because of the indignity inflicted by my own being, because of the impotence that prevented me from saying anything other than a lie: "My tummy hurts!"

My father was not home. My mother asked a neighbor to run over to my godmother, Margarita, a saintly woman who at fourteen had been my own mom's babysitter and later a close friend of hers. My godmother felt me:

"Where does it hurt, sweetie? Here ... or here?" she asked, placing her hand first on my stomach and then on my lower belly.

"Here," I answered, choosing the second.

Big mistake.

They both concluded that I had eaten something terrible but didn't remember what. Or that the milk at breakfast had gone bad. Or that I had swallowed a bug without realizing it. Or that I was constipated from eating half a dozen quince sweets the day before at Doña Ermelinda's store. Or from eating those chicken-shaped bonbons with liqueur centers which were not, to be fair, for children. Whatever it was, something bad had invaded my gut and caused the cramps. Their various conjectures all led to the only possible solution: they put me to bed and gave me an enema.

Not even when the wretched little rubber tube was inserted did I have the courage to tell them the truth. I put up with the humiliation, right till the end. Sometimes fraud is paid for dearly. I understood this on that terrible day, but it was too late to go back. And the farce continued until the very last miserable drop.

I wonder if the divine punishment for lies, or for pride, which prevented me from confessing my weakness, was disproportionate. Maybe it wasn't pride. Maybe it was an exaggerated sense of duty, ingrained at such a tender age, not to disappoint my elders. Repressive family mandates—even if not spelled out, even if only registered in the air we breathe as children—that tacitly dictate how you should be, what is expected of you, what makes up the psychological and social map you have to follow at face value, should be canceled, prohibited by some cosmic law, expelled forever from human relationships.

Thanks to a dose of strength and tenacity, over time I managed to tame my shyness by practicing being the opposite: daring, even impudent, shameless. And this has helped me, if not to defeat the antisocial being I am inside, at least to prevent her from wreaking havoc on my life.

Dissonances I

The priest walked at a fast pace, waving his cassock. Three or four meters behind him was Vitito San Martino, a boy with a certain reputation for being naughty—or at least mischievous—and another chum matching his age and genius. I was walking at equal distance behind the boys, heading to my grandfather's vegetable garden to dig up some potatoes that my mother needed for dinner.

I remember it was cold, and my wool jacket fresh out of the clothes trunk smelled of mothballs. Winter in my town used to be harsh. We woke up with a blanket of frost dressing the gardens and fields in white. My father, like others, used strips of burlap to protect the pipe that carried the water pumped from the well to the tank on top of the house from freezing.

This no longer happens. For several decades now, the water in the pipes, the ditches by the streets, and the cows' water tanks don't freeze. Tropical parrots have come from the north, and other strange birds fill the pampas air with unknown thrills. (Also, people from the north have arrived, evangelist missionaries and other variants of Christianity who, instead of singing Gregorian chants in Latin, play the electric guitar and sing with a microphone in the atrium of the temple, as in a dance club. I have been told that some parishioners like it, and others miss the intimate calm of the Roman liturgy. I guess it's another type of climate change.)

But going back to that afternoon. If there was hardly anyone on the streets, it was not because of the cold, which didn't intimidate those of us accustomed to the rigors of winter, but because the people had gone en masse to the sports club to attend the soccer game, our team against a neighboring town's. Apparently, our priest not only detested movies—he said the cinema only contributed to the impoverishment of our souls—but also that sport in particular, because of the profanities that came out of every mouth and in front of children. It didn't surprise me. This priest was a fine

and sensitive man, as he should be, and he condemned vulgarities. I liked to hear him at Mass singing psalms, with a rich and firm tenor voice, and mod-
ulate to surprising tonalities while the smoke of the
incense filled our lungs with an intoxicating oxygen
charged with sanctity.

And now I saw him walking down the sidewalk
with an air of purpose. Who knows where he is going,
I wondered. Perhaps to visit a sick person, or that dis-
believing family that had not registered their girl for
the first communion. Mine did, God gracious! when I
was seven, although they did it more to avoid clashing
with the rest of the townspeople than out of personal
conviction. To be honest, my father hated the church.
As a child he had attended a religious school in his
hometown. He sang in the choir—he had an angelic
voice—and for that reason, and because he was a very
handsome little boy, he was the favorite of a priest.
This priest used to sit him on his lap and say,
"Juancito, you are such a good child!" caressing him
lasciviously, something my father confessed to us
when he was old. I don't know how far the pedophile's
abuse went but I have no doubt that it was the unfortunate source of the anxieties and nightmares that

plagued my dad for life. If he concealed this story for more than sixty years, he never hid his contempt for the church and their priests. Nevertheless, on Sunday mornings, when families attended Mass, I would settle into my parents' bed to listen to Bible stories. He told them with grace and rich detail, but in the end, he added his own epilogue, finished them off with a dismissive gesture:

"Bah! They are all legends, the things that priests use to fool the fools!"

My mother, on the other hand, without having received formal religious instruction, had a natural affinity with the spiritual world. I never saw her enter a church or pray or give signs of faith. She saw God in the glow of a golden autumn leaf, or in the perfect proportions of a flower, or in musical scales, a concept that I absorbed from her during every piano lesson: a pure and most genuine form of pantheism.

In contrast to all this was my soulmate, Mariana, who professed an unwavering faith in the Catholic religion. Determined to counteract the half atheism half agnosticism of my family, she taught me about the Biblical Word and injected me with divine energy so that I would attend mass and confess often. She even gave me a white, embroidered mantilla. We all know how imponderable the influence of our peers can be at that age.

It was July 1959, a month of freezing afternoons in the southern hemisphere. I remember it well because it was the month when the "infamous Fidel Castro usurped power in Cuba and instituted the communist regime," as our teacher announced to the class the day after the event. From the tone, we thought she was going to cry. But no, she just turned pale. She explained to us that this Caribbean Island would be a springboard for the Bolshevik atheists, enemies of God, to launch themselves into the rest of Latin America. I imagined a bunch of Cossacks lined up in front of a trampoline of sidereal dimensions, making stratospheric leaps and in a triumphal flight diving into the waters of the Río de la Plata. Fortunately, our little town was far from the capital. The announcement filled us with restlessness, and she urged us to go to Mass and pray for our country.

This inaugurated a time of mystical fervor in me, which was increased as a result of an event that propelled me toward the safe path of purity of the soul, with a push from Mariana. Two days before, I had gone to a traveling amusement park with five pesos in my pocket. For some reason I don't remember, I went alone. I spent four pesos riding around on the carousel and other attractions. And when I saw a left-over peso in my hand, I looked around and discovered a sign that announced:

Slides only $ 1.00!

I paid, and the manager pointed to a wooden structure identical to the church pulpit, or so it seemed to me, at the top of which there was a rectangular opening for a viewer, well above my head. I jumped uselessly until the man pulled up a bench and shot me a sideways glance. I climbed up, happy and full of curiosity. I looked through the hole. And one by one, the luminous slides began to parade before my eyes. They were women. Blondes, brunettes, redheads, with red lips, puffy, parted, puckered lips; most of them were semi-naked, just in underwear, very brief, and all in indecent postures.

At a dizzying pace, various erotic images passed through the viewer, although the most forbidden areas were covered by hair falling in waterfalls. The man was pushing the slides forward at a guilty speed, and I barely had time to absorb what I was seeing. Mind you, it tasted like sin. A wave of shame ran through me like dirty water. It must all have lasted no more than twenty or thirty seconds. When finished, I silently got off the bench, murmured a "thank you" in a low voice to the owner of the exhibit and left, perplexed. Only then did I notice the men behind me, waiting their turn. Head down and with tears trembling on my lashes, lamenting the sad fate of my last peso, I headed to Mariana's house.

My misery was palpable, but I didn't tell her about the whirlwind that raged in my head. I just said I was worried about my sick dog. The lie added salt to the wound, and I sobbed. My friend, very devoted by family tradition and temperament, offered me a rosary. I had no idea how to use it; I had never held such a devotional object in my hands, but I murmured a few *Our Fathers* and *Avemarías* as they came into my head. She accompanied me for a few minutes, passing the beads on her own rosary and, from time to time, inserted a prayer for the health of my dog. At last, we both smiled: I, because I realized that prayer had exorcized the Devil inside me; and she, by relishing a soul-saving intervention.

I felt light. If before my faith was lukewarm like a badly prepared *mate*[4], that day I experienced a sudden religious conversion, the kind that occurs when the spirit feels overwhelmed by a growing affliction and at the height of stress becomes receptive to what is being offered as a lifeline. (Later on, I would learn that this peculiarity of mind is at the core of some brainwashing techniques that cults use for their own proselytizing purpose).

Back home, in a spiritual rapture, I wrote a love poem to Jesus, sat down at the piano, invented a melody and improvised some chords in the so-called minor mode, melancholic by nature. And thus accompanied, I sang the first psalm of my own invention, which was more plaintive than the tunes of the Andean Quechuas. Then I tried it on other scales, in intervals of five, ascending and descending, with the rigorous addition of sharps and flats, as required by the natural law of harmonics. I mention these musical details because, already in those days, I was amazed by that exquisite numerical proportion of the notes in all

---

[4] *mate* = an Argentine tea

the infinite scales, even in those we cannot hear. And I had the intuitive certainty—without ever having heard about Plato and the world of forms and archetypes—those tonal relationships and rhythms, like multiplication tables, had not been invented by anyone, but instead inhabited another universal, timeless dimension. There, I felt, they had an independent presence and existence, an abstract reality that I barely made concrete and perceptible with my fingers on the keyboard. Didn't the Scriptures say, "On earth as it is in heaven"? That, to me, explained everything.

This musical exercise relieved my anxiety, because now I had restored—within myself—the implicit harmony of the cosmos.

This happened, as I said, shortly before the day when I was walking behind those two boys and in front of them Father Giuliani, floating on a cloud of religious anointment. His presence was an excellent omen. A warm sun rose from the clouds, and everything was clearer. I was now on the right path, straight and illuminated.

I did not dare to hurry my step. Reverence would not have allowed it, because if I were to pass him, how could I have greeted him? What could I have said? *"Adios Padre"*[5]? Of course not. The words "A-Dios" would be redundant to his most blessed ears.

Vitito had a broom in his hand, and the boys were laughing, who knows what about. What a lack of respect! My soul was in suspense. Father Giuliani was so close, and those two brats behaving that way! Suddenly, Vitito approached Father with rapid steps, and with the end of the broom he lifted his cassock, while saying: *Pollerudo!... Pollerudito!* [6] My heart skipped a beat, and time froze.

The priest stopped short, turned around and faced us, transfigured. How to forget the man's reddened face! It had transformed into a beet, and it seemed that the devil himself was jumping out of his eyes when he said hoarsely, stretching out an arm and pointing at them with his index finger:

"I'm going to kick your ass, both of you!"

Ohhh...

I do not remember the subsequent events, but I do remember the impression of the universe collapsing at my feet, with priest, Jesus, Virgin Mary and all

---

[5] *Adiós* = Goodby; *Dios* = God

[6] *pollera* = skirt. *pollerudo* = somebody who wears a big skirt, mostly a disrespectful and funny reference to priests.

the saints. If he had threatened them with the withering wrath of God, or with expelling them from Paradise, or punished their souls with a whip of burning bushes, I would have understood and even approved. But a kick in the ass? Could there be something more vulgar and banal coming out of the mouth of the delegate of God Our Lord in the earthly kingdom?

It took me the rest of the winter to get over the emotional shock. It had been a disconcerting episode in the most literal sense: the concert of the spheres had been shattered on the ground, unhinged in atonal chaos. And one spring morning, without pain or glory, I simply abandoned the dogma of the church. I dropped it like the butterfly leaves the chrysalis that no longer serves as its support. Whether that puerile slip of the unhappy priest was the cause or not of my metamorphosis, I don't know. Perhaps it was the natural evolution toward maturity, toward independent thinking and introspection.

Even so, this did not undermine my faith in the Platonic dimension from which the laws of the universe emanate in their exact and beautiful proportions, that dimension outside the corrosive reach of time and space.

From then on, at the age of eleven, that was my way of defining Divinity. Even today I try to listen to its harmonic resonances in the manifest world and to make my way through the many dissonances.

Don Col

I was having breakfast on the morning of August 2017 when I noticed the now infamous *New York Times* photo on the table next to my steaming mug and turned to read the article:

The city of Charlottesville was involved in one of the bloodiest confrontations when white supremacists defended the permanence of the monuments of the Confederates in the southern states, which ended with the death of a woman and dozens of wounded.

It was not the very first news item published that year by a US newspaper about incidents between racist groups and human rights activists, but it was the most violent. Perhaps it was the mingling of the aroma from my coffee and the word *Confederates* that brought to mind the peculiar image of Don Col, which fluttered in my conscience with the soft pinprick of nostalgia.

We had known so little about this man, and yet I for one found it impossible to forget his unexpected presence in our community.

It must have been on a day towards the end of the fifties that I was walking with my grandmother down the sidewalk in town when I caught sight of a gaucho coming in the opposite direction. On one side of his sash hung a whip, on the other a knife.

The two grownups must have been more or less the same age. My grandmother, very pale; the man, very dark. He stopped and, taking off his beret, greeted her with a gentle bow of his head.

"*Tudo bem, minha senhora dona Adelina?* (How is everything, Miss Adelina?)"

They talked for a long time in a language that sounded so soft, so pretty, like a rustling of leaves. When we got back to my house, I said:

"Nonna Adela was speaking in Latin with Don Col".

It was a slip of the tongue typical of my age. My grandmother's round belly began to quiver—it was there she seemed to concentrate her virtually silent laughter. I knew that, in the whole village, only Father Giuliani spoke that sacred language. How often had we heard him murmuring its canonical syllables during the litany! He knew them so well that he could enunciate them without stumbling, even while his lynx eyes watched, with vigilant zeal, the altar boy passing the tithe offering bag among the congregation.

"I meant to say Friulian," I said, correcting myself. I was referring to the dialect my grandmother spoke with those of her own background.

"It was neither Latin nor Friulian," they explained, amused. "It was Portuguese." From the conversation that followed between my mother and my grandmother I only remember two words, which sounded in my brain like a stirring of bells plus the rhythm of drums: *campinas* and *capangas*. I didn't know at that time that the first referred to the beautiful region of Brazil where my forebear was born, and the second to a hateful figure from the same country.

Ever since, I supposed the man was a Brazilian gaucho from Rio Grande do Sul. But I had also heard my father say that Don Col must have come from Jamaica or the United States because he spoke English. It was all incoherent detail, and it sounded contradictory to me, but my confusion must have lasted all of five minutes, because I don't think I thought about it again until many years later.

Still, as Borges wrote, *"Only one thing does not exist, and it is oblivion."*

Little could be learned from the man himself, who was taciturn by nature and spoke in the most convoluted manner. His curious appearance is still etched in my memory: a tall, skinny man with a very dark face and gray eyes. He was old by then, or so it seemed to me from the wary perspective of childhood. He had several teeth missing.

He wore a black beret and white gaucho shirt and baggy pants, also always white, with a black sash. He also wore black espadrilles. I enjoyed seeing him walk through the streets dressed like that, with the wind ruffling the folds of his wide pants.

He could often be seen cleaning the ditches on both sides of the street so that the rainwater could flow unimpeded. These were the only storm drains in the town. That's where we would launch our paper boats the day after a storm—the kind that soaked the Pampas and rendered the streets impassable—had filled them with water.

On those soggy days, no one dared walk across the street and risk losing a shoe or getting stuck or falling flat on their backsides in the mud. That was what the narrow, cement pathways at the street corners were for. And to keep them clear was Don Col's responsibility. He would roll up his pants and clean them thoroughly with a shovel.

That was all I remembered of this unlikely character until, by some mysterious association, the *Times* article jostled a dozy nerve in my head where the facts of yesteryear are stored. And I wanted to find out more about him. Where had he come from? Why would a black man, so obviously foreign but dressed in the gaucho style and speaking Spanish peppered with English and Portuguese flavors and perhaps some African overtones, end up in a community of Italians and *criollos*?

In an impulse to disentangle the past (something common at a certain age), I emailed some of my peers back home and learned that their memories were as fragmented as mine. The first question had to do with his name.

Was it actually Col, or Coll, or Cole?

"If he really was from the United States, it would be Cole," someone said, "like Nat King Cole."

"Or Colt, like the revolver," suggested my brother, prompted by his well-justified association of firearms with North Americans.

I favored Col, the diminutive of *charcoal* in archaic English. The name suited him.

As for his temperament, the consensus was that he had been a respectful and respected man, not at all a troublemaker.

"Yes, he was a good guy," someone added. "But, as the saying goes, courtesy does not detract from bravery, and in the case of this good man, his kindness did not take away at all from his courage and fierceness. That's the way of men who are close to the land."

And to prove it, he recounted the following incident: "When Negro Col was still young, one night he hid among some reedbeds, and when an enemy of his came upon him, Col stabbed him. The altercation was over a woman, and the man he stabbed was one of the Domínguez family, a very large and well-known people in the barrio."

The incident was never brought to justice, or if it was there were no consequences. The narrator of this story reminded me that, in the old days, "the police turned a blind eye when dealing with *issues of women.*" He said that the anecdote had been corroborated by two descendants of the Domínguez in question, who had apparently survived the attack.

It is also said that Don Col's seed found fertile ground in the Argentine Pampas, because he fathered a child with a woman from the barrio. I can add nothing more about the individual who bore his DNA imprint if not his name. But it leads me to observe how human history unfolds and people connect in unforeseen ways.

Nor is another anecdote apocryphal because I heard it from a friend who was an eyewitness. His family lived on a small farm not far from town. His sisters had the habit of going out on their own in the evenings to dance at a grocery or liquor store, the kind that could be found in the Pampas in the middle of nowhere, where the gauchos used to gather to socialize, dance and drink, or fight. But at my friend's farm there was a ferocious dog belonging to a farm laborer that frightened the girls when they returned late that night. They complained about it to their father, and he asked Don Col, who was working for them at the time, to take care of the matter. We do not know if something was miscommunicated between the two, or if the boss gave his worker carte blanche. What's certain is that the next day the animal was found hanging from a tree.

Again, the Confederates come to mind. Today I wonder if the memory of some lynching, a common thing in what was possibly Col's homeland, would have emerged from deep in his consciousness, and prompted this act, so unknown in our culture. *God, who saves the metal, saves the dross...*[7]

Regarding Don Col's origins, various theories were put forward. Some claimed he was an American on the lam, others the son of Brazilian ex-slaves. Yet others say he was a castaway on the *Principessa Mafalda*, from the Italian coast of Liguria, which in 1928 sank in Brazilian waters near Bahia (a tragedy that came to be known as "The Titanic of the Atlantic"). Due to the vagaries of the ocean currents, he

---

[7] Argentine poet Jorge Luis Borges, *Everness*

ended up on the banks of the Río de la Plata. I eliminated this theory, however. The years may have coincided, but not the geographical distance, or the human cargo, or the *Mafalda*'s route.

At last, I found somebody whose recollection was trustworthy and intact: my cousin, Ricardo, who I turn to whenever I want to recover a lost childhood memory. His version is plausible because Col often spoke not only with our nonna but with my cousin's father as well as with another mutual friend.

"Not Col or Cole," my cousin said with an air of authority. "His real name was Robert Colt, a native of the State of Tennessee. You know, one of the most racist places in the United States at that time."

Yes, I knew about that. Then Don Col, or Colt, had grown up in a state where public places, buses, schools, and even drinking fountains, were segregated. The lynching of African Americans in the streets, for a petty crime or false accusation, drew a lively white crowd that celebrated justice as prescribed by the white supremacists. Colt was the grandson or perhaps the son of slaves, who as children had been taken from their families to be appraised and sold in the public market, who were passed from family to family, perhaps crying, perhaps with the sad meekness of the oppressed. Always in despair.

Don Col would not have forgotten the face of pain.

My cousin continued, "One fine day he went to New Orleans to scrub boats. That didn't last long."

This seemed feasible to me. In that key cotton port, there would always have been jobs on offer for stevedores. But staying there would have been unpalatable: black men were treated no better in Louisiana than in Tennessee.

What's more, the difference between these African Americans and the others—the Afro-Caribbean descendants of those who had come from Haiti with French masters fleeing the Haitian revolution—was obvious and would have caught Don Col's attention and perhaps opened his eyes to another kind of freedom. Haitian slaves were not under the yoke of the Protestant religion, which determined and sanctioned their subservience in the social order by promising happiness in the hereafter. Unlike those born in North America, the Haitian slaves generally did not adopt the religion of their masters. The Caribbean black people of French New Orleans, like their predecessors in

Haiti, were free to congregate and celebrate a syncretic faith that merged—or I would say absorbed—the numerous Catholic saints and their own African deities, so they emerged as revered entities in their own right. Perhaps Don Col had witnessed regional voodoo and Santeria ceremonies, which might explain his acquired taste for dressing in white? Perhaps this fueled his desire to assert his own identity.

"He got tired of New Orleans," my cousin continued, "and decided to look for a better life. He stowed away on a boat. This was in the thirties or thereabouts. The man had balls! I admire his courage."

"So he came to Buenos Aires," I asked, "from New Orleans?"

"No, no. The ship was going to the port of Santos in Brazil. And, since he didn't know Portuguese, he was sent to a plantation where English was spoken."

"English? In Brazil? Are you sure?" I asked.

"I don't know. I'm just telling you what I heard from my dad."

Suddenly an image started flickering on the edge of my mind. I groped for a name in the darkness until it came to me: the Vila Americana! It was no coincidence that the article on the Confederates had reminded me of these names. My subconscious would have made the connection between the Portuguese name and the late nineteenth-century American slavers based in Brazil. Or maybe the information had been engraved in my memory because my grandmother had at some point mentioned the community, which had established itself shortly before her family arrived in São Paulo?

I confess that I enjoy the thought that it was Don Col's spirit whispering in my ear through some cosmic channel.

"Are you referring to Villa Americana in São Paulo?" I asked Ricardo, elated by my sudden insight. I am always in awe of the intricate fabric into which the threads of human destinies are woven.

"I have no idea. I know it was Brazil."

When I lived in Rio de Janeiro, I read about a place where the founders' Anglo-Saxon traditions were celebrated every year. The city, which was just a villa at the time, harbored some ten thousand Confederate Southerners, slave owners who, after having lost the Civil War in the north, had emigrated to Brazil "planning to maintain the institution of slavery," as some articles claim—and others deny. In any case, they clearly meant to continue planting cotton and also try out other crops: coffee and sugar cane. It was just a matter of buying land and more slaves. They had the know-how, and Brazil had not yet abolished slavery.

The diaspora was received with the enthusiastic approval of the Emperor of Brazil Pedro II (who paradoxically was called "The Magnanimous"). And there is no doubt that some of these cotton barons brought their ex-slaves with along them, in addition to their language and their Presbyterian religion, between 1865 and 1885.

"I think it was in the Campinas region. He used to work there picking coffee," my cousin explained.

Campinas! The word echoed in my mind with a familiar chime. That's where our grandmother had been born and raised. How many times had she told us about the huge, dark, and terrifying underbrush surrounding the coffee plantation! I imagine her walking among the coffee fields, with a headscarf or a hat woven from palm leaves to protect her sensitive skin from the tremendous tropical sun. Her family, the Fanin, was from Friuli, from the snowy mountains where Italy rubs shoulders with Tyrolean Austria; and they were brought to replace the labor force of the newly emancipated Brazilian black slaves. And in that massive wave of migration, which at the end of that century so profoundly shaped our Americas, my grandmother was born ... right in the Campinas region of Sao Paulo, perhaps only a few kilometers from where Don Col worked the plantations.

I had left so many questions behind in the inkwell of childhood indifference. And today I find myself questioning the ghostly shadows of my elders.

At the age of fifteen, my grandmother left the farm in an ox cart with her family. After traveling through one dark jungle after another, circling estuaries and struggling with swamps where they were often trapped, they finally arrived in the most hospitable of Argentine lands. A decade later, she would meet Don Col on the street in our small town in the Pampas, more than two thousand kilometers from his native Campinas, and they would greet each other in Portuguese. They would start a conversation about memories, perhaps recalling bare hands reaching into bushes to retrieve ripe coffee beans, under the stony gaze of the *capanga*, the intimidating foreman who was used to managing slaves with a whip.

The ways paths can cross never cease to amaze me.

"According to this Mr. Colt," my cousin continued, "he eventually left Brazil seeking to better his lot in life in one of the boats ferrying "swallow" migrants (so called because they did short runs following the harvest season). In Santos, he again boarded one as a cook, this time for Uruguay, with the intention of getting to Argentina and working during the corn harvest. And that's what he did. In Buenos Aires, he took the train to another province and got off here, at our station."

At this point I must bring in another piece of the story, narrated by yet another reliable source, an old *criollo* who met Don Col when he already had a small ranch in the next barrio over from his house. According to what Col told his neighbor, the treatment of black people in Brazil was better than in Tennessee or Louisiana, but not the pay. He had exchanged one pittance for another. And equipped as he was with an intrepid soul, he decided to continue south. Without money, he walked for days to reach the port of Santos.

"The man walked from the interior of São Paulo through the jungle to the coast. There were poisonous spiders, huge snakes, even jaguars! But also a large quantity of fruit. Sometimes he would kill an armadillo, or a bird, with a sling. And then he would build a small fire."

"Those same things that the gauchos knew how to do when they roamed the Pampas with empty stomachs, high and dry, as they say," I added.

"Yes, they were resourceful. They were clever. We *criollo* men have the knack," the man said with a somewhat melancholic expression.

And then he continued: "On the ship they were packed like sardines. There were white men, black men and mulatto men, a bunch of workers who came to harvest the crops, make a few pesos and return home. But Don Col was not going back. He had no homeland. It was like he was searching for it... He said that the night before the shipwreck he had dreamed of the Pampas, and a huge blue sky that curved over the plain and protected people of any color.

"What shipwreck? It couldn't have been the *Mafalda* as some people think," I observed, "because that ship came from Italy."

"No. This accident happened in Uruguay, off the coast of Rocha, near the mouth of the Río de la

Plata. You travel a lot, so maybe you know the place? It seems to be cursed, rather like the site where a ship has gone down—where compasses don't work and vessels go crazy, or so I've heard. Fact or fiction, who knows? But Don Col told me that when he realized they were sinking, because they had run aground on the rocks, he did not want to be dragged down by the whirlpool a ship creates as it sinks, and he just jumped into the sea. He swam and swam until he reached the Uruguayan coast. The coastguard found him and some of the others on the beach. And since this black man spoke oddly, and they didn't understand anything he said, they didn't know what to do with him, so they put him in a mail van with instructions to get him on another boat bound for the port of Buenos Aires. There was an immigrant center there, I mean, several of them, because there were so many Italians, Poles, Croats, Basques, people coming from everywhere... There they fed him and loaded him on a train that went north, I think to Tucumán, after handing him a note he could not read, where they had written an address and the name of the owner of a brick kiln who needed workers. But when the train passed through here, Don Col said he liked the golden fields so much, and the sky was so beautiful, just as he had dreamed of it, the very same, that the landscape got into his soul, and he just hopped off and never left."

"So he got off on impulse!" I exclaimed. I was moved.

"Oh yes. My grandparents have seen many people come from abroad because they had heard good things of the town and the fields. And not just from Italy. The Turks and the Armenians came; others from Bosnia, like your teacher's family, the Kovasevich... Who knows how many there were!"

"My grandfather was one of the first," I reminded him with some pride.

"Yes, one of the first to come from outside. Because we *criollos*, we have always lived here. Always. Since God created the world."

My informant was partly right. His predecessors, at least on the indigenous side, were already prowling the Pampas well before the Spanish arrived in Argentina in search of a way out to the Peruvian *argento*. But his Andalusian eyes denoted a more complex ancestry.

"I didn't know about the shipwreck," my cousin said when I mentioned it to him, "but what my father did tell me is that when Don Col got off the train, he went straight to the police, and the commissioner, Fernandez, gave him protection. You see, there are decent people everywhere. And from then on, the municipality gave him free accommodation in a cell that was always unoccupied, in exchange for keeping the ditches clean."

The act was not overly generous from our present perspective, but it was perhaps the best one could hope for from a community of Italian settlers in a remote place in the mid of the last century.

Later, in my day, he earned the title of "Don," once he began to comb gray hair.

I went back to the newspaper article, trying to weave together the loose threads of this story. I decided to think like a detective, dusted off my best Portuguese, and wrote to a descendant of the Confederates in Villa Americana, asking him to check the town archives from the 1930s. Some days later, he confirmed that, yes indeed, a worker named Colt who had hailed from New Orleans had been there.

I took the opportunity to ask my São Paulo source if it were true their North American ancestors had brought their black servants with them.

"Yes, it's true that a few came bringing those who had been their slaves," he wrote. "But it was not to prolong slavery. It was well intentioned. Mind you, freed black men had nowhere to go after the Civil War. They were practically unemployed. Suddenly they were left alone, disoriented, without the protection of their masters. They themselves asked their employers to bring them here to Brazil. They wanted to remain under their protection. They came voluntarily. "

Voluntarily? Of course, they were already free men, I thought. But his whole assertion is questionable. We don't know the circumstances. We do know, however, that Robert Colt shaped his own destiny, defying what has been decreed for him by other men.

I like having met him. And I am glad I have started to revisit the past. When I go back to the town, I will look for him in the graveyard. He is buried, I am told, as one of our people.

In the meantime, I read on the Internet the following article from Brazil's *Folha de São Paulo*:

August 20, 2017. Hundreds of people participated in the annual festival celebrating the 1865 arrival in Villa Americana, of ten thousand

Confederates. Statues of these pioneers adorn parks and gardens, where the Confederate flag snaps proudly in the breeze.

And in the *New York Times*, a less happy commentary:

August 20th. President Trumps' Thursday morning tweet laments the removal of Confederate monuments, which "tears apart the history and culture of our great country." This raises numerous questions, among them: just who is he referring to in that "our"?

What exactly, after all, is the "history and culture" that is being torn apart?

The speckled hen

My grandfather entrusted my brother with euthanizing the speckled hen. Ax in hand, he said, in his thick Italian accent:

"It's easy. With one hand you grab her firmly by the body, and with the other you whack her on the neck with this, and *listo!* But watch your fingers!"

My brother needed no further explanation. Those laying hens have black and white feathers so he could easily spot her from afar among the others, some of them red and some pure white, like the snow on the Andes mountains.

I'm not sure why my brother recruited me for the grim task. He showed up with the ax in tow and handed me a paper bag with corn kernels, saying he needed help luring the chicken. But there may have been other reasons. Perhaps he wanted to show off his bravery. There are countless opportunities for a brother to show off his talents to a little sister. Another possibility, which seems more plausible to me, is that he was scared to death.

"Why do you have to kill her?" I asked, more out of apprehension than curiosity.

"Because it has avian pest, that is, and we have to eliminate it before it infects the others. Do you understand?"

"Why can't *Nonno* do it?" I insisted.

"Because his knee is really bother him today, and he can't walk all the way there.

Our grandparents' house was just five blocks from the land where Grandpa kept chickens in an orchard behind our father's business. It was a considerable distance given our grandfather's arthritis. Today I know it all too well. If my brother inherited his gregarious character and taste for partying, I was the one who got his osteoarthrosis in my right knee.

"Why doesn't he ask *Nonna*?" I insisted again. "She knows how to do these things".

"No, she doesn't. Don't you remember what happened to her with the firewood?"

I didn't want to remember. But the mind cheats you sometimes. I mean, many times. It puts up fences and entraps you. The more you try not to imagine a scene, the more stubbornly it replays. And that incident still makes me shudder to this day.

My grandmother had been chopping wood for the stove—this was before she acquired a kerosene range—and she missed the log by a hair. The ax caught her foot. She said that at the time of the blow it didn't hurt at all. She took off her shoe expecting to see a bruise. The tip of her middle toe was missing but she didn't notice until she shook the shoe and the severed flesh fell to the ground. Only then did it begin to bleed and hurt. The most curious thing about this story is the laughter that overwhelmed our grandmother when she told us the story. "Imagine," she would say, "a toe falling out of my shoe!" I was not amused, but nevertheless we had asked her to show us the truncated digit.

The task we had been assigned was definitely not a fitting job for either grandparent. That is why, in the absence of a more sensible voice and since there were no adults in the house, I couldn't refuse to give my brother a hand, literally speaking.

I carried the bag of corn; he, the executioner's instrument. I was the accomplice who would lure the condemned, and he, the executor. Or at least that's what I thought. We were already nearing the place where the death penalty would be carried out when he explained that my role was not just to toss the corn and make the hen follow me to its final destination. I also had to help him hold her, he added, because he was going to need both hands to deliver a strong blow for the beheading.

I protested. This was manipulation. He resorted to a dirty trick, that is, to the infallible bribery formula: when we returned, he would do my arithmetic homework, a worksheet full of fractions that I was extremely worried about.

The fruit trees in the orchard were all citruses: tangerines, oranges, grapefruits and lemons. And that spring day, the fragrance of orange blossoms was so potent that it almost masked the odor of chicken coop. The most agile chickens napped on the branches, among the glossy dark green leaves. The heaviest, on the ground, under its shade. The speckled hen was a big one, the kind that couldn't even fly to the first branch.

My brother, always creative, found some bricks and put together a makeshift execution platform. He explained that the blow would be most effective on a hard surface. A knot began to form in my stomach. Then he went into the garage where work tools and old bicycles were kept and unearthed a burlap sack. He walked to the lemon tree while I distributed corn to distract the flock and not arouse suspicion. I wanted to take a deep breath to calm my nerves, but a chicken coop is not the best place for that.

"Cluck-cluck, cluck-cluck"

They swirled around me. It didn't take my brother long to toss the burlap sack on top of the hen and carry it to the sacrificial table. My skin broke out in goosebumps.

With its body wrapped and its head sticking out, the hen stretched its neck and cackled intermittently, with a harsh and strident sound.

"Come. Get a good hold on her and don't let her escape. From here, see?" said my brother, indicating where to hold her, "but be careful! Don't put your hand near the neck!"

I obeyed. Gripping her through the burlap, I held down the hen tightly. I wouldn't let her slip away.

The unsteady pounding of my frightened heart mingled with hers. Her whole body was beating like a small imploring drum.

My brother wielded the ax. I didn't have the courage to look and wanted to close my eyes, but I thought of my grandmother. Self-preservation dictated that I watch the path of the ax.

"Do it!" I yelled.

I was pressing on the animal more and more, and the cackle, muffled by my hands, became unnerving.

But it was he who didn't have the nerve to look. He closed his eyes (he would later say he only narrowed them) and delivered the blow. There was a crunch of bones. I screamed. The ax didn't hit the neck, but lower, in her thorax, a few inches from my fingers. The hen gave a hoarse, exhausted croak.

"Oops!" was all my brother managed to say when he lifted the burlap.

We were shocked. The unfortunate, battered animal was making a tremendous effort to get up. The hen struggled to her feet and stood for a second on her legs. Then she tipped over, dizzy, and collapsed. She lay there, like faint, looking directly into our eyes, with opaque pupils and an open beak. My brother dropped the ax.

"We screwed it up," he murmured.

"You missed her neck," I replied with a tremor. I remember (or imagine) a sincere expression of remorse on his face.

A light breeze rustled the leaves of the fruit trees. We looked at each other. We didn't know what to do confronted with such agony.

"We have to get *Nonno*," my brother conceded after a while, "so he can finish the job."

Exhausted, we covered the hen piously with the burlap. From the slight undulation under it, we could tell that she was still alive. I was stifling a cry. At last, we ran out of there, with a sour taste in our mouths.

Our grandfather hobbled the distance from his house to the orchard. We accompanied him with long faces, tottering alongside at the same pace. When we reached the henhouse, we led him to where the dying animal lay.

"*Per Cristo!* What have you done!" he exclaimed in Italian when he saw the disfigured hen under the makeshift shroud. Her *élan vital* had fled the body.

And what was once life was now an inanimate mass of flesh wrapped in feathers and already surrounded by flies.

Muttering in his language, from which I only understood the blasphemous expression *porcaritá*[8] (a euphemism that has nothing to do with "charity" but with the Madonna), our granddad put the still warm corpse in a bag and threw it over his shoulder. He asked us to pick some tangerines (*do something useful*, he must have thought, though he didn't say it) and take them to his house.

Back home, I prayed that there would be no chicken or chicken soup for dinner that night. By chance, there was not. My mother emerged from the kitchen with a steaming plate of corn quiche. The mere sight of corn kernels made me nauseous. Claiming a lack of appetite, I nibbled on a piece of bread. (There was no way I was going to make the terrible mistake of faking a stomachache again)[9].

The episode is doubly significant to me for two reasons. First, for the disturbing experience of having

---

[8] *Por carita* = for the sake of charity. It is a play on words with *porca*, a very blasphemous adjective to the Virgen Mary.
[9] A reference to a previous story *The cure*.

a life under my hands and being an accomplice in its death. Of course, before, long before, I used to sacrifice insects and snails without batting an eyelash. I would look for them in the garden, dip them alive in a bottle of alcohol until they were stiff, and then arrange them in a row, one bottle after the other, in order of height. They were my students. A stick served as my pointer, while I gave them arithmetic lessons or instructed them on Evita Perón's newly founded *Children's City*.

But a chicken is light years different. I had felt in the palm of my hand the trembling of her entrails, the clamorous pulse of her warm blood, like an ancient rough sea. I had seen her watery gaze, heard her last cry.

The second reason that I find this incident significant is due to my brother's comment a few days ago, when I wrote to him asking for details to complete this narrative. Surely, he would remember it better than me.

"The story is true," he wrote back. "I remember It. But you were not there, sister. I was alone that day.

"Are you kidding? You forgot! I was there! I see can that hen as if it were yesterday," I replied.

"No, you weren't there. You can be certain. I re-member that you were very affected by my story and you didn't want to eat anything for dinner. Just a slice of bread".

One of us has created and saved a false memory. It could be him. It could be me. It is not un-usual to attribute to yourself something that hap-pened to a close person, or to recall someone else's dream as your own. But the opposite is not unusual either: forgetting the presence of another.

Truth slides toward the imaginary, changes its sign and meaning, changes owner and name. Is it a sensory trick, to make sure we "remember" an event in a way that favors us? Or just a flaw in our fallible perception of the world, susceptible to persuasive voices or images implanted from outside? The passage from the real to the perceived is not a stone bridge, firm and stable: it is a fragile one and, when it breaks, reality dislodges. Don Quixote saw Mambrino's hat; Sancho saw a saucepan. The man fell into the river. The eyewitness saw who pushed him. "I was there. I saw it," the witness would say. His or her eyes saw branches swaying in the wind and the inverted mirror of the mind reflected murderous arms.

My brother and I killed the speckled hen. My involvement no longer exists in his memory. Or, on the contrary, he told me a fact and I reconstructed it in the privacy of my conscience, giving me a presence at the event. And today I recreate it as such.

Dissonances II

According to the historians, the idea of demarcating the town in the shape of a triangle came from the rancher who donated the land.

As girls, neither Mariana nor I found that geometry strange. We believed that all communities followed the same design as ours and that the triangle was the basic geometric property of small places. Mariana thought that squares were reserved for cities, where everything was ordered and legislated. I put in that circles befitted cities that were both mystical and mysterious.

My father, who had come from a city, liked to say that some joker must have wanted to prove Thales of Miletus' theorem on the layout of a town. However, in catechism class we were informed of the real reason: the triangle represented the Trinity, and that is how our town's donor and benefactor, a deeply religious man, had wanted it. Other reasons of a more practical nature, like hectares and stuff like that, were alluded to only in passing.

I didn't understand that whole business of One in Three and Three in One... It was hard enough for me to grasp the idea of two Gods, the Father and the Son. To think in terms of three was beyond my mental capacity, not to mention that they were three inextricable persons, and that the third, the Holy Spirit, sounded like a spook to me, if not a downright nightmare. When I asked the teacher on duty at Sunday school about this, the answer was always the same: the Holy Trinity, at whose vertex was God, was the Great Mystery, and I should stop asking questions and overthinking things. Mariana begged me to put my heart into my faith, pure and simple.

So I got used to not questioning anything, at least not out loud, and to channeling my concerns into making art. I was the one who came up with the idea of designing the town following that divine blueprint, and from then on, we spent our evenings at Mariana's house, working at a table covered in paper, pencils, rulers and erasers.

With the ruler we drew our triangle and then, crossing it and running parallel to one of its sides, the railway tracks, which cut the area in two: a smaller triangle and a trapezoid. Then, on "our side" (the small triangle) we drew four streets parallel to the tracks and another five parallel to the other side of the triangle, the one that led to the west. The latter, naturally, ran diagonally to the railroad tracks. At the end of the lines appeared sixteen blocks that were neither rectangles nor squares but rhombuses, as if a telluric force had pressed and distorted the natural quadrilaterals. There were also some residual triangular blocks on the third side of the triangle, where the parallels and diagonals died out.

The trapezoid that remained on the other side of the tracks made up the so-called barrio. It lay behind our triangle, its geography somewhat too diffuse for us. There we drew a small lake, a plaza, a pasture and a paddock, and nothing else. We knew nothing about the streets or the people—the *criollos*—in the barrio.

Mariana's father said that the town was not exactly like that, full of rhomboid blocks, but that was what our drawings produced. And we liked it that way. A diamond, after all, is made up of two facing triangles, and this fact had its symbolic and representational role in what the triangular totality was (today we would call it a fractal phenomenon). Either way, everyone knew about our oblique streets, which were unavoidable in such a layout, and this unique arrangement created corners at acute and obtuse angles that were called "ochavas." Another proof of the power of eight! I thought, like musical octaves, which always go back to the beginning.

Once we had finished the ground plan of the town, we wrote in the three powers of the Trinity—the Father, the Son, and the Holy Spirit—in the respective angles of the great triangle.

One day, this sparked a theological discussion. The Father, of course, enjoyed His supreme position at the apex. It couldn't be otherwise given the patriarchal society we lived in. I think it corresponded with the soccer field, more or less. The Son was inevitably located below and to the right, that is, at the right hand of God, as the Scriptures say. And, from our perspective, this coincided with the entrance to the town, where years later, if I remember correctly, they erected two very pagan obelisks in the Egyptian style. This meant the Holy Spirit, who ended up at the cheese factory, occupied the left corner, that is to the left, or in the Biblical language, "*a la siniestra.*" And this sounded horrible, because "sinister" applied to murderers, monsters and communists—the Leftists. So, we decided then and there that right and left, or *diestra y siniestra,* would apply only to objects in straight lines, such as birds perched on electrical wires, rather than to geometric figures. This reasoning put an end to our byzantine discussion.

Finally, we drew the last street, one that emerged from the triangle and led straight to the cemetery, without *ochavas* or turns and returns.

When our layout was ready, we set about marking all the significant places. Her house, my house, the school, the train station, the church, the post office, the funeral home, the agricultural cooperative and, finally, the four corners where the cinema, the bakery, the pharmacy and a clothing store faced one another. There was no bank. This was the commercial center, not the geographical one, since determining a central intersection in our design was impossible. Even more impossible than squaring the circle.

Instead of words, we used icons: an ear of wheat marked the bakery; a skull, the funeral home; two hands intertwined, the cooperative; a cross, the church. Last to find its place on the map was Mariana's grandmother's house because it was outside the formal perimeter and where the fields began. We drew a heart.

Townspeople like us didn't get lost in this quirky place. Both of us had been born and raised among the rhombuses and triangles. But outsiders certainly did! Some were commission agents who brought parcels from the cities, or sales representatives who went from business to business with their briefcases full of samples. Others were grain buyers and middlemen. And then there were the newly arrived residents like a first-grade teacher who always got confused and walked around with a compass.

To complicate matters, no one referred to the cardinal points in order to orient themselves because these were relative. The north of town, for instance, was almost never directly north but northeast or northwest, depending on where you stood, as Einstein would perceive it. People simply said "towards the railroads" or "towards the church." We kids used these terms when we wanted our backs scratched. "Towards the plaza ... now, towards the school" were classic ones.

Father Pietanesi was a newcomer. He had come to replace Father Giuliani for a short time, and he always looked lost because these landmarks were not part of his mental map. He was about the same age as Mariana's father, but he was not mustachioed or dark-haired like many of the Neapolitans in the area. Like Father Giuliani, this priest was blond, with a rosy cherubic face, eyes as blue as the Tyrrhenian Sea, and a captivating voice besides.

It was clear that he was from a family descended from northern German Italians. Everyone knew that the further north in the boot you went, the closer to heaven you got. People who looked at him felt ... I don't know how to describe it. After all, he was the one who spoke with God, according to Mariana. Well, maybe not with God himself, but with His divine messengers. She had heard her uncle say: "The new priest talks to the angels at siesta time."

And this made sense, I thought then, because people used to say: "Ah ... for me naps are sacred!" In any event, the angels will give full attention to Father's prayers because at that time of the day all the adults were snoring like pigs.

It is true that, on more than one occasion, the priest had asked Mariana where So-and-So's house was, and she had guided him through the confusing diagonals with a "Follow me, Father," which was all she dared utter.

He never spoke to me, though.

What happened that summer's day my friend told me several years later, after our two families had moved away to the city.

One day Mariana had the urgent need to see the Father speak with the angels, or at least listen to him doing so. The night before we had seen a Spanish movie, *Miracle of Marcelino*, which the new teacher, an exemplary product of a convent school, had highly recommended. We all cried our eyes out at the end. But Mariana had returned to her house highly moved, she told me, her soul aflame with exaltation, pure and holy, like that experienced by St John of the Cross in his mystical poem, "Dark Night of the Soul."

Like Marcelino, she longed to speak with Jesus or, if that were not allowed, at least with the angels; although, if possible, without dying like poor

Marcelino. But how to summon those glorious beings? The film did not explain by what means the Lord had appeared to the boy. Surely the secret lay in the bread and the wine, she thought. A voice inside her head began to make itself heard. Its terrible and absolute command: "Go to the house behind the church and see how Father Pietanesi invokes the angels. See it with your own eyes. Hear it with your own ears."

Next morning, my friend told me, she woke up with the movie's soundtrack on her lips and a steel-like resolve. She did not share this with me or anyone else but waited until church service ended at noon and Father would have had his lunch. Soon it would be siesta time. Businesses were beginning to close their blinds. People yawned. The grownups withdrew behind heavy shutters and ample curtains, while some boys sat on the cool tiles of a porch to talk quietly or play marbles.

At one-thirty, when her parents had also succumbed to the sweetness of sleep, Mariana tiptoed into the kitchen, poured some red wine from a demijohn into a small jar, and sliced a hunk of bread. She wrapped them in a napkin and placed them into her sisal bag, which she put across her chest. Then she walked briskly toward the church.

A low white sky weighed down on the town. It was that empty time of day when everything seemed to stop in the drowsiness of the afternoon: words, steps, even breathing slowed. A warm breeze occasionally stirred the leaves of the trees, and it too smelled meek.

Mariana knew the churchyard well. We both had helped in the garden with other girls from school—countless times! An ancient tree stood behind the priest's house. Called a Paradise Tree, it was laden with intensely scented lilac flowers. She would have to climb up to the top branch, she realized, because it was an old-time building, and the window was too high for her to reach. Intuition told her that Father would be behind that window in his room—and not in the kitchen or dining room, because neither place was conducive to invocation.

Today I wonder if I would have been as fearless as Mariana. I don't think so.

With the stealth of a mountain cat, she placed one foot on the first fork of the tree and then the other, and soon found herself in the shelter of the dense foliage. Her heart was beating fast. On the afternoon air wafted the friendly smell of incense, which soothed her [like a balm] as she breathed it in and out.

A bird flapped its wings, so that shadows fluttered overhead, and then settled on a branch nearby. It was a little, red-breasted meadowlark, small and tender like an angel's soul. A small chirp broke the silence. Mariana heard a welcome in the innocent trill; she smiled at the lark and continued to climb up cautiously but surely.

I am not surprised Mariana remembered all these details even years later. As time goes by, scenes and conversations are even more firmly shaped by memory, as if the most lucid part of one's being insists on not forgetting.

From this leafy vantage point, she finally had a clear view of the window. "How lucky the curtain is open!" she said to herself, as she sat on a branch ready to spy without being seen or heard. She didn't feel a bit of guilt because her motives were genuine. The All-Knowing who looks into children's souls from above knew this too. At first the mirror of an antique chiffonier was all she could see. She had not thought Father Pietanesi would go in for that kind of furniture. Well, it was obvious that the house had been furnished before his arrival by one of the parishioners, Mariana mused, or by the previous Father, the one who had gone off to the Bahamas for a spiritual retreat.

She waited. Father was nowhere to be seen. Was she too late or too early? But every now and then the breeze carried a low whisper like a prayer. It was possible that he was in some corner out of her sight. She changed position, choosing another strong branch to sit on and watch from a different angle. Holding onto a branch with one hand and using the other to open her bag and take out her offering, she suddenly saw the priest's silhouette reflected in the mirror.

In one hand, he held a chalice, which he raised to his lips before offering it to someone standing in front of him, whom Mariana couldn't see. "An angel!" she said to herself, and her heart pounded.

She heard agitated sighs but could not make out the words. As she craned her neck to see better, the mirror reflected back something else. She saw it from behind: the priest's hands slowly sliding down a naked back and then up under the skirt of another figure. Mariana recognized her dark, wavy hair, and the color of her skin, white as marble. And her voice: "Don't stop, *Padrecito*, don't stop!"

As Mariana jumped, a groan escaped her. The priest came to the window, closed the curtain and then the shutters. Caught between incredulity and fear, she staggered, and was about to fall, but held on just in time. The meadowlark flew away from the tree with a frightened chirp. She clambered down quickly, not seeing where she was stepping but obeying a terrifying instinct that took over and guided her feet.

She felt an intense pressure in her chest. She was four feet off the ground when she slipped on bird droppings on a branch and, losing her balance, fell face first to the ground. She didn't know if the harsh cry that stirred the birds came from her own throat or from the crow that lived in the garden. With the taste of dirt and blood in her mouth, she ran to the gate and, without turning to close it, kept on running until she reached her grandmother's house beyond the triangle, where diagonals went to die.

She went around to the well in the backyard and leaned herself over the edge to pour the stream of images besieging her mind into the dark waters. But she was assailed by her own bloodied image rippling on the surface. With both hands, she pulled hard on the rope and lifted a bucket of water up to the edge. She dipped her hands in the cool water and washed herself again and again.

Her grandmother heard the peculiar sound of the cord in the pulley and the song of the bucket being lifted as water spilled from its sides.

"What's wrong, my dear?"

"Nothing, Grandma. Look, I brought you some bread and wine from home. But then I fell and my bottle broke."

"You cut your lip!"

"It's nothing. Do you know something, Grandma? Father Pietanesi doesn't speak with the angels like Uncle Tito says he does."

"He doesn't?"

"No. I saw him. He talks to Miss María de los Ángeles[10]. The teacher."

"Hmm, dear...! And what was she doing at the priest's house?"

"Maybe she was looking for another house and got lost..."

---

[10] Ángeles = angels

"Um, maybe. Who knows, Father Pietanesi might be right when he says that those diagonals are things that the Devil uses to confuse people."

Years later, when Mariana left town, she took its strange layout and its subjective cardinal points with her—and also the memory of a brutal summer afternoon when she learned something about the surprising geometry of the human soul.

Since then, she told me, she looks for a town where the streets run straight, and outsiders do not get lost. Or if they do, then at least they do not walk down the streets of duplicity.

If I have related two similar experiences concerning two parish priests (similar not because of their degree of seriousness but because of their ups and downs, their moments of fervor and disappointment), this is not due to a twisted taste for this sort of thing. It is just a reflection of life, which insists on stubborn repetition.

The cistern

I have a clear memory of the day when Mr. Saltanelli threw himself into the cistern. That the man drank excessively was known, but no one imagined this ending. Saltanelli had left an empty bottle of red wine on the edge of the tank. "Perhaps to give himself the courage to take the last leap of his life," my mother commented. It was also reported that two men with a ladder had descended into the well. Working together they lifted the inert body from the water and then rose to the surface, one holding the deceased by the head and the other by the feet. Some say they hauled him up with the rope, like a bucket of water.

Who knows. There are things that belong to the collective memory of a people, and this includes

questionable happenings and uncomfortable questions. The truth is that they had taken Mr. Saltanelli
straight to the funeral home to dress him and make
him look good before the wake, as I heard the green-
grocery's daughter say. To me it seemed impossible
that he could make a presentable appearance, because the faces of the drowned are not placid, nor do
they wear calm expressions with smiling lips waiting
to be welcomed to the celestial world. "Anyone knew
that!" I dared to say.

"But that does not matter!" the girl corrected
me. "Drowned or not, our souls are all welcome in the
Kingdom of the Lord if we have been good. The problem is that the soul of this deceased remained in the
well," she added, and crossed herself. I was more than
taken aback.

After this disastrous event, the Saltanelli family emptied the house and moved to the city. They put
their dwelling up for sale, but as expected, no one was
interested. And so the property remained unoccupied
and at the mercy of the grievances of time.

A year later, the situation took a most unexpected turn. The piano and typing students from my
mother's academy had already gone home. She and I

were listening to a Palmolive soap opera on the radio when the bomb fell.

I must clarify that even at the end of the fifties there were no telephones or televisions in the town. The radio, with its glass tubes that radiated a strange warmth, was the only thing connecting us to the heartbeat of the world. That afternoon they were broadcasting an emotional episode of *The Children of Nobody*, a series that drew tears even from the mirror on the dresser. Just as the narrator proclaimed that two orphaned siblings had been kidnapped by a black-souled harpy, we heard a knock at the door. My father went to open it, and there was Commissioner Manacordes, whom we called Mangascortas[11], standing under the two bronze plates at the entrance, one for the *CIMA Typing School* and the other for the *Conservatory Scarafia*.

"The Commissioner wants to speak to Horacio," my father said from the door.

My legs wobbled with fear.

My brother was just eleven years old. Suddenly I realized that kids, too, had to answer to an authority

---

[11] *Mangas cortas* = Short leaves

above the paternal one, a force that didn't emanate from the holy power of the church but from someone rather mundane.

The Commissioner had a revolver, while the other junior policemen had batons hanging from their waists. I never saw them punish anyone, but perhaps the mere sight of the club and the gun was enough to make everyone walk the straight path, or as straight as possible in a town as skewed as ours.

My father invited Mangascortas into the hallway and right there the Commissioner asked my brother if he was involved in what had happened in a house on our street street. And Horacio, bravely, said "yes."

I knew who had cooked up the scheme and why. My neighbor La Chuli had apprised me. According to her, the Saltanelli's was a haunted, demonized house, inhabited by an evil so violent and of such a nature that it had to be uprooted by another act of the same degree of violence. She had approached me as an interested party. Because that ill-fated house was, I'm not saying attached to mine, but with a neighbor in between still close enough to affect me. What she didn't tell me at the time was that my brother was a member of the exorcism team.

I could only see the haunted house's garden, which was a mess of bad weeds, and the oranges and tangerines rotting on the ground. But those who knew it from inside claimed that, although small, it was a pretty house. Its smooth ceilings were not at all like those of my house, where you could see the long hardwood beams supporting the white painted bricks forming the roof. Of course, these bricks were interesting to observe at night when lying on our beds, because they had recorded the tracks of chickens and dogs when, still in their molds, they were left to dry in the sun. But interesting is not synonymous with quality and good taste. Moreover, the courtyard of the Saltanelli home wasn't filled with primitive dirt soil like many others but covered with decorated tiles.

In short, it was a well-finished house. But that hadn't protected it from being cursed. And it was precisely the most beautiful detail of the home's construction, something exceptional—and, I think now, obsolete—that caused its ruin: the cistern.

It could be seen from the sidewalk, between the bars of the fence. The rounded edges were covered with tiles of the *Talavera de la Reina* type. Most attractive was an ornate wrought iron semicircular arch, culminating in a floral motif. There was the pulley and sheave that a rope would have passed through in earlier times, before there was running water in the house and when the cistern was not a mere relic. Or a grave, like now.

"As I told you, there's a grieving soul in the house," Chuli told me.

"What is that? "

"A saddened, hopeless soul... a ghost."

And to validate her theory, she took me to speak with Don Salmán, a Christian Lebanese shopkeeper and the priest's right hand.

"It's true" Don Salmán confirmed. "There are spiritual entities wandering among the living, without a definitive resting place so they are not in peace, and this happens when the body they inhabited in life doesn't go through a proper burial."

"But it wasn't like that with Don Saltanelli," I argued, "because he's in his coffin in the cemetery, buried as the church mandates, and the grave even has a bronze plaque with his name on it. I know it for sure, because my dad sold it to the family."

"True, but the ecclesiastical canon affirms that the souls of suicides are denied entry to heaven for having violated a sacred law, which determines that if God is the one who gives you life, He is also the one to take it away, child."

His words left me speechless. It seemed to me an excess of authoritarianism on the part of God, an inexplicable injustice, on a par with the denial of paradise to unbaptized babies. I had taken for granted that spirits return to the First Cause (a dimension devoid of such harsh rules) from where all Being emanates, no matter how and who ends their biological life. It now dawned on me that my gnostic vision of the divinity (which I had picked up who knows where and, guided by some innate tendency, adopted without qualms as a parallel belief to the official one) was not in tune with the prevailing Catholic dogma. I suppressed the sacrilegious thought, packed it up and put it in the bag of doubts to be clarified later in life.

The displeased chatter of the townsfolk went on. This spirit who lived in the cistern made life miserable for us, the living. It (he) would come out of the depths every night and prowl, I was told, not only around the poor man's former abode—perhaps with a certain nostalgia for domestic life, I thought—but around the neighborhood, sowing problems. And neither Chuli nor the others wanted it (he) wandering around. For them, it was the beginning and origin of everything bad that happened to them: if they lost a ring or an earring, it was the soul's evil at work. If their stew got burned, it was blamed on the phantom's misdeeds. Surely this evil apparition should be expunged.

For me, after all that hubbub, Saltanelli's ghost was a source of night terror, when I lay awake, scared to death by the moving figures in the shadows. One in particular was a projection I saw on the window with changing contours: hands, feet, mouths, all threatening forms. By day they were the innocent lemon tree branches in the garden. At night they were the demons of my lucid insomniac hours.

The result was that when my brother joined the "cleaning operation team," I interpreted this literally, like an exorcism accomplished with soap, water and broom. But it was not like that at all.. One day at siesta time, when the sun was beating down on the tin roofs of the sleeping town, they invaded the abandoned house armed with sticks, stones, and painting supplies. Emboldened by the arrogance that a gang confers, they wrote profanities on the walls in red ink, broke tiles and window glasses, and smashed mirrors—mostly mirrors, because they are known to hold mysteries. They filled the toilet and sink with gravel to plug the pipes and, of course, they vented all their rage on the cistern. From the sheave they hung a doll with pins stuck in the belly, and then they threw broken bricks into the well, at this point full of toads and stagnant water. They did it for the good of the villagers, they said.

I only learned of the extent of the vandalism that afternoon when the police arrived and the next day, when they took the six perpetrators to jail.

And so began their two-week sentences, which followed this routine: At eight o'clock in the morning, conveniently after breakfast, a guard would collect the boys at their respective homes and one by one escort them to the police station. At seven in the afternoon, when the night shift began, the miscreants were returned to their families for house arrest.

The police station consisted of an office facing the street and a large courtyard behind it, enclosing a kitchen, a bathroom, and a cell. Every day, the six prisoners had to sweep the dirt patio, water the soil to settle the dust, and clean the kitchen. Those with exemplary conduct were allowed to serve *mate* to the Commissioner and the other guards. If anyone rebelled, he was sent to sweep the sidewalk. Passersby would stop to point at him, laugh, and then continue on their way, shaking their heads. My brother was spared that humiliation, perhaps because he was the son of a teacher, perhaps because he knew how to ingratiate himself with the Commissioner, employing the brilliant rhetoric that has always distinguished him.

That Summer, the so-called heroes of the Saltanelli case were imprisoned for the last two weeks before classes started. Unfair thing, it was said among the convicted ones, because theirs was an act of extreme courage that fulfilled its mission. The ghost had fled. My neighbors confirmed this because after the day of the exorcism there were no more strange accidents in their houses; and I, because the nocturnal appearances stopped in mine.

After this harrowing episode, I began to think of those who commit suicide, who turn off the light of life for the last time. And of those who kill themselves little by little with alcohol. My mother sometimes recited the famous poem *Lo fatal*, by Rubén Darío[12], and I had memorized the first verses:

Blessed is the tree that is barely sensitive
and more so the hard stone,
because it no longer feels;
and the last ones:
...with no knowledge of where we're bound
nor from whence we've arrived.

I wondered if Don Saltanelli had also suffered from an incurable disease, like Darío. Then he would have had the right to kill himself without incurring divine wrath. Or if, perhaps, he was a poet, one of those who drink to mitigate the senses and the anxiety of not knowing where we are going, or where we come from. In which case, I thought, I could also invoke the right for anyone to kill themself, because at the moment of Death, according to my optimistic cosmogony at the time, the secret doors of Truth are opened to all, and all mysteries are clarified. All the knowledge of the finite or infinite universe would be given to me and to

---

[12] Poem title translated as *The Ominous* or *Fatality*

all mortals, good or bad, holy or sinful and all in between.

It was a strange conviction.

As for the prison sentence, only decades later I learned that it had been decreed without the intervention of any judge, without a trial, without a verdict, and without any written records filed in the Courts of Justice. It was an agreement between the Commissioner and the parents of the vandals. The owners of the house objected to such a light punishment. In order to settle the matter, the boys' families offered to pay the heirs for their expenses.

In the end, the house got cleaned; the owners satisfied; with the soul of the suicide resting in well-deserved peace; and the well, duly exorcised.

Tango Night

Until the year I left the town known as María Susana, and during its fifty years of existence, we were aware of only one murder, one armed assault and robbery, and two suicides. Because the murder occurred in the *barrio* and took place within an Arab family, very few remember it today.

The assault, on the other hand, was the worst scandal—apart from those crimes that defied the rules of decorum—because the assailants and the assaulted were well-known people. And one of the suicides was tangentially related to that dramatic event.

This narrative is a reconstruction based on Dr. Posada's memoire, on the burglars' confessions, and on my own memoires of that night of tango.

As usual, two orchestras from our neighboring

towns had been brought in to enliven the evening. It deserves to be clarified that in past decades the town had supported a local ensemble. Poorer villages might make do with a phonograph, but these contraptions were not for a farming community like ours, which could feed entire cities. The original group—a quartet made up of double bass, a violin, an accordion, and a piano—played foxtrots and tangos. Their music appealed to the interwar generation of immigrant children, born and raised under the flag of this country and deeply attached to its uniqueness—mate and tango. Their Spanish was loaded with colorful expressions from the dialects of the Italic peninsula.

The original quartet I'm thinking about was formed in the late 1930s and ceased to exist for various reasons, including the natural death of the violinist, the systematic drunkenness of the accordionist, and the marriage of the pianist, my mother.

But at the time of which I speak, a good fifteen years after the end of World War II, the community had prospered even further and was able to hire two musical groups from outside, thereby satisfying the old as well as the new tastes in the population. The "traditional" ensemble played tangos and milongas;

the modern one performed boleros and other imported genres. Both orchestras included singers.

On those tango nights, nobody could escape the voices, dramatic or romantic, which saturated the atmosphere of the town and beyond. No one slept until two in the morning, from pleasure or displeasure it made no difference. From eight o'clock in the evening on, the streets began to fill with pedestrians and cars coming from the farms and other surrounding towns. These pilgrimages from other places by single men and women often led to marriages, which enriched the genetic soup of the respective communities. It was a parade of Dodge Sedans, Plymouths, and other brands—all hard to pronounce. The Fords of the thirties, and even the Ford T, were common among the most tight-fisted farmers, who refused to update their models. But the most ubiquitous in the countryside were the Ford A's. Naturally, the locals came to the dance on foot, because this was a town you could walk from end to end in ten minutes.

For the two thieves who chose that night very wisely, the commotion was not a setback, quite the contrary. Unlike other perpetrators of clandestine acts, who seek protection from shadows and solitude, this pair welcomed the comings and goings of cars and crowds. Stillness and silence do not contribute to anonymity in a small place where people know each other from afar by the way they walk or wear their hats. As we all know, houses have eyes and detect any strange movement on a quiet night on an empty street, like a cat waking up to the smell of a mouse in the distance.

For this reason, the best way to go unnoticed was to make yourself invisible in the crowd of revelers piled up outside the Social Club. And nothing better than a night like this, packed with vehicles coming from the four cardinal points—or, rather, from the three entry points—since María Susana was known for being a triangular town.

Like everyone else, Cholo Rattero and his accomplice Raúl Roble knew that early that week Dr. Posada had received a good sum in cash for the sale of a slightly used car and that the doctor had not yet gone to the bank in the city to deposit the proceeds. They were also aware that Posada's wife, and their daughter of marriageable age, were already on their way to the dance. Because the doctor—according to his own confession—detested both cloying bolero and tearful tango (he had to deal with his own depression, he said), he would be alone, reading at home.

El Cholo had bet and lost all his savings on a horse. A tip he'd been counting on didn't pan out and he needed to get that money back fast or there would be no marriage—a serious matter, since he was now engaged. His buddy Raúl, on the other hand, was a chronically poor man with perpetually empty pockets.

Driven by such urgent needs the two conspirators parked the coupe in a long line of cars a block from the festivities and headed toward the doctor's house. The cold of the autumn night explained their scarves, which when combined with the fallen brims of their hats, made them indistinguishable from other passersby. They saw a light shining in Posada's window and slipped into the property through the driveway.

Once in the courtyard behind the house, they took two masks out of a bag, covered their faces, and pulled their hats down to conceal their eyes. The townspeople did not lock their doors at that early an hour—a custom that still persists—so the pair easily entered the house through the kitchen, using the service entrance.

A moment later they kicked in the living room door. Indeed, the doctor was sitting in his chair reading by the light of a table lamp. Cholo pointed the revolver at him, a Colt 45. Raúl brandished an Italian-made pistol.

"Easy, doctor, easy", said Cholo, nervous enough for the gun to shake in his hand. "We just want the money. Now!"

They say that under his mask, Cholo had his mouth covered with a piece of perforated cellophane to distort his voice. The other had not bothered: the timbre of his voice was so peculiar and twisted that there was no way to falsify it. Instead, Raúl chose not to part his lips.

The doctor dropped the *Selecciones* from *Reader's Digest* on his lap and his eyes widened.

"I don't have it. You can check everything if you want to waste your time," he finally blurted.

"Come on, doctor! Either you tell us where you have it or we blow your brains out!"

The doctor rolled his eyes. He didn't believe them. These two amateurs wouldn't do him that favor. But when Raúl placed the gun at a dangerous distance from his bald head, the doctor noticed how the guy's finger was trembling on the trigger and he sensed danger. The truth is he had no idea who these two could be. The cellophane trick worked well, and Cholo Rattero's piping voice gave him no clue. Posada concluded that they could well be outsiders, braver boys than the local ones. A reasonable voice told him that it was necessary to spare his family the horrifying spectacle of his brains spilling across the carpet.

"It's in the hospital safe," he said with a sigh, placing his brandy glass on the table under the lamp.

"Come on, the keys! From both the entrance and the safe!" demanded El Cholo in his funny voice that came out sounding more like a sheep's bleat than a lion's roar.

With forced calm, the doctor rose from his chair and opened a drawer in his desk, fishing out a bunch of keys.

He was about to extract the two that belonged to the hospital, when Raúl snatched the entire key ring out of his hand and made a sign to Cholo, like someone cutting off a head. The other got the message.

"If the right keys aren't here, I swear you're going to pay dearly. I mean, your wife and your daughter when coming from the milonga".

These two are from around here, the doctor thought angrily. "There *is* no other key ring. This one here is for the hospital door, and this small one opens the safe," he explained. "I hope you at least have the kindness to leave my brandy bottle alone!"

El Cholo put the key ring in his pocket and Raúl proceeded as they had planned. He tucked the pistol into his belt, removed a rope and tape from his bag, and imperiously motioned for the doctor to sit on the chair in front of the desk. With several wraps of the rope, he tied Doctor Posada against the backrest, his arms glued to his sides. Then he lashed the helpless man's feet together and taped his mouth shut, as he had seen done in the movies. The doctor took a deep breath and glared at him with hatred.

Back in the courtyard, the thieves exchanged their masks for scarves and carefully surveyed the street before heading to the car. Despite this precaution, a couple crossed their path. The burglars greeted them with light touches of their hands to their hats, without stopping.

Meanwhile, at the club, the sound technician

had turned on some recorded music to encourage the crowd while they waited for the musicians to appear.

The female voice from a vinyl disk began to sing *Cambalache*:

> *That the world was and always will be filth,*
> *I already know...*
> *In the year five hundred and six*
> *And in the two thousand, too.*
> *There always have been thieves,*
> *Traitors and victims of fraud,*
> *Happy and bitter people*
> *Gentlemen and false.*

I imagine Raúl and Cholo getting into the car, each with a slight smile on his lips as they light up their cigarettes. In three minutes they would have reached the street that marked the perimeter of the town, beyond which lay the open fields and then the hospital. According to later accounts, they parked behind an abandoned barn on the side of the road. Although it was an unpopulated area, they pulled their scarves up to the height of their mustaches and wore their hats low, without turning on the flashlight. It was prudent not to give away their presence, even to the owls.

On the other side of the fence, drawn against a horizon recently swallowed by the night, they saw the vague silhouettes of horses sleeping on their feet. Closer by, something glowed brightly.

"The evil light!" Raúl exclaimed.

"Don't be a fool," the other scorned. "It is the phosphorescence of a cow's skull, shining in the moon's light."

This dialogue was later shared by Raúl, to prove that in the end he had not been a fool. Moreover, as proven by what happened next, the presence of the evil light was entirely consistent with events.

The two continued their trot, approaching the hospital.

I was already at the dance when the technician put the record on the victrola and the strains of the ultra-romantic *The Day You Will Love Me* came alive in the air. The audience converged on the dance floor, arranged in their customary groups according to gender, age and interests. Toward the back, young men, standing or sitting, well dressed and with slick hair, drank beer and ate peanuts, dropping the crushed shells to the ground. Not far from them, the young ladies were seated. They were accompanied by their mothers, aunts, and grandmothers, all drinking anise or egg liqueur as they anxiously awaited the beginning of the dance, already on the lookout for invitations delivered with a nod from a respectable distance.

The married men formed a bouquet of hats in a corner of the club, where they could be seen smoking and drinking. There was no doubt they were talking about their favorite topic. Whoever thinks that this was the wheat or meat price for export—the products that lubricated the world's machine in those parts—is wrong. What consumed their passions was the result of the most recent horse race. The comments were the usual ones: all variations on the turf theme, such as how the stallion was three-quarters English blood, or the mare that finished last had tendinitis.

The children ran around in the middle of the yard, pushing each other or playing tag. My friends and I, all preadolescents, huddled in our usual hangout, an uninhabited area behind the bandstand, waiting for a modern rhythm to encourage us to dance among ourselves.

That night, a traditional orchestra had been

hired from the neighboring town of Armstrong, or *Armistron* as we called it, a legacy of the strong British presence in the country. The announcer took the microphone and asked the children to clear the floor. The dance session was about to begin.

His amplified voice made our eardrums shake, and reverberated, metallic and robust, off the walls of the vast room. The words came in overlapping waves of echoes that only trained ears could decipher.

The musicians entered the bandstand and tuned up their instruments. The singer tested the microphone with a "hello, hello," and was satisfied.

At the other end of the village, the thieves heard the announcement and quickened their pace. That night the smell of burning hung in the air. The farmers had set fire to the stubble to prepare the fields for sowing and a gust of wind brought the would-be burglars some fine ashes. It also brought them the first verses of a very popular tango, *By a Head of a Noble Horse,* that the singer attacked from the start with a deep vibrato as the opening theme.

Cholo almost came to tears, Raúl said. What irony of fate! The same thing had happened to him! He was referring to that "fucking horse," as he put it, the one on which he bet all his savings only to see it lose by a head! And him by five thousand pesos.

They soon found themselves in front of the hospital. It was a white, rectangular, single-story building surrounded by tall eucalyptus trees. The roof glowed silver under the moon. At one end stood the water tank, with a red cross painted on each of its four faces, and above it, a pole flying the Argentine flag. The hospital did not keep patients overnight; the seriously ill were transferred to the city. The thieves also knew that no one was guarding the clinic, since there was nothing of value that was portable enough to steal.

They put on their gloves. Raúl inserted one of the keys into the lock on the front door, which opened into a small reception area. Locking the door behind them, El Cholo turned on the flashlight. On one side, a corridor led to a community pavilion with a row of beds and some bathrooms. The other side led to the doctor's office. The place was not strange to either of them. They had come out of here once, clinging to blue blankets and sucking on their mothers' breasts. Now they were back, after twenty-something years, clutching revolvers and sucking on cigarettes.

They headed for the right-hand corridor, with the flashlight beam bouncing off the white walls. In the middle of the hallway, Raúl tripped over a badly parked metal table that rolled on its wheels until it collided with the wall. A vial with an unknown liquid exploded on the tile floor. The noise raised the hairs on the backs of their necks, and the smell sent them into a sudden panic, like someone about to be operated on without anesthesia.

Outside, the wind began to blow more vigorously and shook the branches of the eucalyptus trees.

At the club, the canvas above the dance floor shook several times. Nobody was fazed. The orchestra continued its performance with a well-known tango, *La Cumparsita*. It was an ideal piece to showcase one's talents. Several middle-aged couples and others of more advanced age took the floor. Straight torsos, intertwined legs, chest to chest, or in many cases belly to belly, showing off their improvisations and dexterity like mimes bragging about their art.

The young people had neither the interest nor the ability to master tango choreography. They hoped that this "outdated thing" would soon pass and the "danceable" one, with its cha-cha-chas and boleros would start.

After the scary moment, the partners stopped in front of an open office door. They inspected the interior, shining the flashlight. Nothing there. They continued to the second door, the one to the doctor's office, which stood ajar. Standing under the lintel, they watched with uneasy eyes for a few moments before entering. The beam of light showed a well-nourished library of chunky tomes on the opposite wall. Raúl would later relate how he turned the flashlight to the left and jumped: hanging from the ceiling there was a complete human skeleton, smiling at them from above. On the walls, illustrations of the lymphatic and circulatory systems completed the decoration. With some caution, they entered the office. El Cholo quietly opened the window and poked his head out. There was not even a dog outside. But the stanzas of yet another song made popular by the great Carlos Gardel came to him clearly:

When you slit your shoes
Looking for that buck to survive...

He closed the window with another smooth movement, reminding himself, uncomfortably, that the soles of *his* shoes were also about to expire.

A solid oak desk occupied the center of the office. To one side stood a model of a human spine made of plaster. In the center of the desktop—on a sheet of paper lined up on the roller of a Remington typewriter—some notes had been typed beneath the heading: *Pancreatic Cancer: Symptoms and Treatments.*

"There it is, Cholo!" Raúl whispered excitedly, as the flashlight illuminated a metal vault.

Strapped in his chair like a roll of stuffed meat, Dr. Posada had his eyes fixed on the pendulum of the clock hanging on the opposite wall above the desk. He was counting the beats that pulsed in his jugular: one hundred twelve, one hundred fifteen, one hundred twenty. Blood pressure couldn't be measured, but he sensed it. He was short of breath and felt a pain in his chest. Well, if he died of ventricular tachycardia that same day, the agony in which he had lived for some time would end. No more sleepless nights. The rope had tightened around his wrists, and he occasionally moved his fingers to ensure circulation. But something else tormented him, the alternation of two conflicting feelings: a vengeful desire versus a righteous conscience. Where was his moral integrity? Why did he plant those words in the heads of those petty thieves when they were leaving? What gave him that awful idea? This is something he would confess to later in the memoirs he left to his wife.

The wind changed direction and crept through the semi-open skylight, bringing with it the first staccato notes of another tango that people loved:

> *Now downhill on my roll*
> *Those past illusions*
> *I can't tear them off ...*

Dr. Posadas would have given a finger chopped off his hand to stop hearing that irritating and pounding music that was another facet of his polymorphous torture. He remembered the prisoners of war, forced to listen to the same song loudly, twenty-four hours a day, as a method of brainwashing. But was it true, or did he read it in a novel and it was just fiction? This fogginess of his brain was a sign of poor oxygen. He took another deep breath.

The wind was playing tricks on him and he could close neither the window nor his ears. He thought about reproducing the first chords of Beethoven's Seventh Symphony in his mind, using the internal sounds to override the external ones, because he knew that sensations--real or imagined--are all inner perceptions. But the Allegretto movement he loved so much immediately metamorphosized into the Argentinian national anthem. He blasphemed. The words screamed in his throat and piled up inside his sealed mouth. In desperation, he focused on generating the angry sounds behind the duct tape and making them rumble inside his skull. He perfected the technique, and it did him good. As if by magic, he calmed himself down for a while. Then, the anguish of a tremendous urge to urinate began, as he would later divulge to his friend, the pharmacist.

There was, however, another equally vexing anguish, one he confessed to later. His heart beating with repentance, he wondered what those two jerks might be doing.

Exactly as the doctor feared, on the other side of town the thugs were about to open that nefarious strongbox.

Raúl inserted the smallest key in the lock and turned the cylinder. The safe's heavy door opened without the slightest sound. And there they were: five tall bundles of thousand-pesos bills, which would add up to a total of ...

"Twenty thousand bucks!" Exclaimed Cholo, who was as quick with his eyes as he was with his numbers.

In a second, they had the bundles stashed inside the bag and were about to close the vault when Cholo, wanting to make sure they hadn't overlooked anything, asked Raúl to light up the interior again. And then he saw it.

"Look what's here, buddy!" From the back of the bottom shelf he retrieved a beautiful bottle of expensive brandy. "He likes good stuff... and he hides it, the naughty doctor!"

"He might be afraid the nurse is gonna' steal it!" Raúl joked. "Well, come on, man, we have to get out of here".

"Wait a bit, let me wet my throat, as a reward..."

"Come on, asshole, it's getting late," Raúl said,

uneasy.

"Yeah, yeah, don't get on my nerves."

The musicians took a break. On the ladies' table were plates of peanuts, french fries, and olives. The women chewed and chatted.

"And how is the doctor? someone asked Mrs. Posada. "He seemed a little depressed the other day."

"He's okay, a bit of a hypochondriac lately, but fine, unless you count his prostate problem. He goes to the bathroom every fifteen minutes."

"Why doesn't he have surgery?"

"He's terrified of the scalpel."

Suddenly another gust of wind shook the canopy above the dancers and the lights went out. A chorus of "oooohs" spread through the room.

The announcer appeared with a megaphone and called for calm. The couples used the darkness as an opportunity to kiss with passion. A few minutes later the light returned, and several men were caught with their hands where they shouldn't be. There were some blushing and clearing of throats, spilled wine glasses, and gestures like someone adjusting the knot of a tie, like "nothing happened here."

"Let's go, Olivia, it looks like a storm is coming," said Mrs. Posada to her daughter.

"No, wait a bit, Mom, the modern orchestra didn't even start!"

The mother didn't insist. The singer resumed his performance with another popular theme:

Goodbye, friends, companions of my life,
beloved group of begone times...

In Dr. Posada's hospital office, Cholo collapsed, dropping the ominous bottle of brandy, which shattered.

"I told you, idiot, not to drink!" Raúl yelled at him.

With his eyes rolling, his lower lip trembling, and a tragic grimace on his face, Cholo clutched his stomach with both hands, writhing on the floor.

"What's wrong with you, man? Tell me!"

Cholo Rattero could not articulate a word.

"He's dying! He's dying!" Raúl told himself. "What the fuck was inside that bottle! Oh, Virgin Mary!! Give me a hand, tell me what to do!!

Get out of here! a voice told him. According to

Raúl's account, he was not sure if it came from the Virgin Mary herself. In any case, he obeyed, taking the bag with its purloined contents and running away. He'd gotten as far as the hallway when a thought stopped him. "Shit! They'll think I killed Cholo for the money! They are going to charge me with murder!"

The air carried the last verses of the *Adiós Muchachos:*

All the parties are over for me.
My sick body can't resist anymore!

Raúl retraced his steps and threw down the bag next to Cholo, who was writhing in pain on the floor. "Better to leave the bag and wash my hands. I don't want to get involved with a dead man!" he reasoned.

He exited again, striding down the hallway, and when he reached the reception area he could hear Cholo's plaintive voice chanting.

"Help me ... help me ..."

Doubt took form, coming and going at the edge of his mind. His steps shortened and grew hesitant.

"...Don't let me die..."

Raúl turned on his heel and returned to the office, where he was confronted by Cholo's wide, pleading eyes. Sometimes Raúl knew what he had to do, after meditating. The ideas came to him in waves, one after the other, but calmly, and he weighed them. Other times, the "epiphany", as he referred to those moments of lucidity, surprised him like a thunderbolt. And so it was that night. Later he confessed—not to the judge but to a friend—that it was not his conscious decision, but something inside his head that did his thinking for him; at some junction in a circuit of his neurons a decision had been made, without him participating in the process. It was very strange!

"Hang in there, brother! I'm going to get the doctor!"

Raúl ran out to the car and started it, pressing the accelerator pedal all the way and fleeing like a condemned man escaping from hell.

The music floating in the air from the festivities brought tears to his eyes:

Return ... with withered forehead,
the snows of time have silvered my temple...

He sped through the oblique streets of that eccentric town, where the outsiders got lost and sometimes the insiders too. He lunged, spinning, almost suspended on two wheels against the hairpin turns, honking at every corner with a screech of brakes, heading for Dr. Posada's street. He parked inside the garage, slamming on the brakes an inch from the wall. Then he sprinted to the back door and came in yelling:

"Doctor, doctor, Cholo is dying! Come on, save him please!"

But the traveler who flees, sooner or later
Has to stop his steps.

"I'm going to untie you, doctor, right away! Pardon us! Pardon me!"

Tears ran down his face as he listened to the singer intoning the last verse:

I keep hidden a humble hope
Which is all the fortune of my heart.
Return... with withered forehead...

When the commotion passed, and the day came

when each one involved gave his deposition in the district court, the judge asked Dr. Posada why he had dissolved poison in the brandy, and why he kept it in the safe. The doctor explained that the mixture was a scientific experiment, and that he had hidden it to avoid accidents. The judge pressed him and asked him about the purpose of such an experiment, and Posada replied that it was a trap to kill the hospital rats, which had lately developed a taste for that particular brand of cognac. Therefore, the dose of the poison was small. Otherwise, the stomach wash he performed on Cholo Rattero could not have saved him.

Cholo and Raúl were given light sentences. The first, because the shock of coming face to face with death, according to the defense attorney, had permanently reshaped his character. Raúl's guilt was mitigated by the noble gesture of not letting his partner die. The two told the story in detail, and it is said that, at the end, they cried, sorry for their misdeeds, (or perhaps for their audacity) in front of the judge, and their repentance had moved him. It also helped that Dr. Posada did not press charges.

Three months after these events, it came out that the doctor's statement had been false. He confessed this in his memoirs. The cognac, he said, did not contain rodenticide but a powerful poison that, diluted in alcohol, tastes good and kills quickly, provided a full bottle is swallowed. But since the concoction had been lost during the robbery, the doctor was left without his preparation and had to resort to another method to end his life.

The pancreatic cancer he had discovered a few weeks before the night of the assault was already consuming his remaining days. One morning he was found dead in his office, with an empty syringe beside him and some sheets of paper detailing the reasons for his suicide and the technique used. He also gave instructions to forgive any debts that his patients owed him. He was in his early fifties.

"A solution used in the euthanasia of animals, a mixture of anesthetic and other powerful drugs that paralyze the center of respiration, causing rapid circulatory collapse, was injected into the abdominal muscle," reported Zaeta, a pharmacist deeply knowledgeable in equine physiology. "The amount was enough to kill two horses!" he added.

On the day of the funeral, the whole town went to church, and the *barrio* people flocked to pay tribute to this good doctor who never billed those who could not pay. As they stopped in front of the coffin, two ladies lamented, "Poor doctor, so many babies he brought into the world, and now he's the one leaving it. Rest in peace!"

"Yes, God have him in His glory."

"Requiescant in pace."

When my turn came, I said quietly, "Have a good trip, doctor, and thank you."

After all, he had been the one who brought me into the world, eleven years before.

The Christmas Lottery

Tonino, the village Fool, was a lanky, gangly man. Everything about him was long and skinny: his body, his face, his hands, his brain. He spoke in monosyllables and gesticulated a lot. They said he was stupid because his parents were first cousins.

"Nonsense," some opined. "He would not be the first. Look at the telegrapher," they'd say, "a Candelo married to his cousin, a Candela.

(I must clarify that the feminine ending of the woman's name, *Candela,* was an invention, a nickname that was kind of a town joke. You see, the girl's maiden name was *exactly* the same as the one she took from her husband, them being grandchildren of the same grandfather.)

"And see how their son turned out normal," argued the various defenders of these anomalous relationships.

"But hey, it's not the same," my uncle Alfredo reminded them. "In Tonino's case, not only his parents were first cousins. His grandparents were also related."

"Yes, but they were only second cousins," argued others.

"It doesn't matter. The defects accumulate, they are amplified. And if you don't get mental defects, there are always other diseases. Have you not heard of the cursed heritage of European blue blood? The British royal family, the Bourbons, the Empress of Russia... All of them suffered from hemophilia due to consanguinity."

My uncle's reasoning left them speechless for a while. A few, I suppose, because they didn't understand what he meant by consanguinity— but most of them deferred because Alfredo was the accountant of the agrarian cooperative, and his words counted, so to speak.

"But, if Tonino is stupid," someone, at last, commented, "Why does he sometimes seem to have clairvoyant powers and forecast things correctly? Do you remember when he predicted the number that was going to come up in the lottery, and he got it right?"

"Yes. And I was so stupid not to buy a ticket at the time!" said another who went by the name of Abelardo.

"True. I read that fools sometimes have a streak of genius, especially when it comes to numbers and probabilities," my uncle continued. "It's as if they had statistics in their heads."

"Too bad that Tonino doesn't like to be peppered with questions. If you ask him about numbers, he sends you to hell. Or he doesn't answer you. Not even his mother can pry his secrets out of him. They could be rich!!"

"Well, he's dumb. Mysteries of the human mind."

"Only God knows..."

I witnessed this animated conversation in the Venice bar, on a hot afternoon, when my friends and I were enjoying an aperitif at the tables on the sidewalk. What sweet times, those! Mr. Septentinelli, the bar's owner and father of our dear friend Claudia was

a very responsible man. He served us vermouth with plenty of sparkling water, accompanied by a plate of french fries and peanuts to mitigate the effect of the drink. At eleven years old, one doesn't have much tolerance for alcohol.

What happened later etched this entire exchange in my memory.

Tonino would have been in his early thirties at that time. He was not exactly autistic, as we would call him today, nor did he exhibit the traits of Down syndrome. I don't know what the diagnosis would be. At that time, our vocabulary only had one word to designate his affliction: "retarded," a word that is no longer in use today due to its derogatory connotation. But back then it seemed appropriate because the boy never learned how to read or to behave socially. He looked at the girls, dazzled and almost without blinking, in a state of pure rapture, with his mouth open and a trickle of drool running down his chin. He dared not speak to any of them, much less touch them. He was a respectful person.

It was clear, however, that his neurons were wired in strange ways. For example, Tonino would often join a group of men hanging out and talking next to the pool table at the coffee shop. And at one point, he would fall asleep. I am not saying that he would literally "fall" while he slumbered, because, in fact, he did not drop to the ground. He would simply close his eyes, snore a little, and remain standing up—with a slight oscillating movement and without losing his balance—like the flame of a candle when the breeze hits it, as if there were an internal, flexible shaft tied to his shoes. After a few minutes of sleep, he would open his eyes and join the world of the awakened to the best of his capability.

"Tonino, what were you dreaming about?" They would ask him.

"About Mrs. Panchita's cow," he would say, or something like that. People paid attention to his dreams, with the hope—already somewhat exhausted—that he would deliver a premonitory lottery number.

Our town's "contrary" lived with his mother, a widow. In the summer, he would sit motionless for hours in a wicker chair. When a fly came near, in a flash he'd catch it with one hand. One fly after another he counted and then let go. He surely hunted the same fly over and over again, but that was inconsequential for his maniacal purposes. What he measured was not the number of insects that entered the house, but his own concentration and dexterity.

Tonino was meek as a lamb with the townspeople but extremely hard on himself. They say that one day he was changing a car tire, a job that he knew how to do well. But this time, while hammering a stubborn washer to loosen the wheel, he accidentally smashed his finger. He screamed and got so annoyed that he raised the hammer and hit his own head hard and fell unconscious.

Tonino didn't go to Mass. The priest wanted to lure him into his herd, but the fellow resisted—and if his mother tried to drag him by one arm, he would scream like a pig being led to slaughter.

"Tonino is not stupid," muttered my uncle, a convinced anticlerical.

People treated him with affection and respected him. But Abelardo, a good saddler who nevertheless detested his profession, invariably chased and harassed him. "Tonino, Tonino! Tell me a number!" he would demand.

The Fool would usually make a dismissive gesture with his arm to shake him off, like a botfly, and continue on his way. If truly annoyed, he would turn around and yell, in his mother's dialect, "*¡Imbecille!*"

At other times, his answer was utterly cryptic, not without a certain poetic touch, such as, "You will have to count the daisies from Don José's field."

Who knows if he wasn't doing it on purpose, just for fun. He was one of those who acted out of intuition in the moment, not by obeying the demands or whims of others, especially Abelardo, who was so obsessed with the lottery.

According to the story later told by Tonino's mother, one hot day of the week before Christmas, when the sun's rays filtered obliquely through the branches of the weeping willows in their courtyard, Abelardo passed by and saw Tonino through the fence. He viewed him from behind, sitting on a log that served as a bench. The Fool was as still as the afternoon. (Here I would like to add that Tonino's immobility, according to my uncle, was dynamic. He occupied the same place, yes, but at different moments of time; ergo, there was movement.)

Mostly from routine or habit, Abelardo stopped and called to him from in between the slats in the fence. "Tonino! What number?"

To his surprise, this time the Fool turned to him with an enigmatic expression, and shouted, "Eight thousand nine hundred and ninety-nine!"

"God bless you, dear Tonino!" Abelardo exclaimed, extremely excited, his eyes wet with pure joy. It was a magnificent figure.

Muttering the numbers while moving his lips and pounding the digits into his saddler's head so as not to forget them, Abelardo flew to the shop of Mr. Di Celio, the undertaker—who also sold magazines and lottery tickets—praying to God that the number, or at least one with the same numerals at the end, was available. And indeed, it was! A true miracle, because it was *La Gorda*, the Christmas draw, the biggest lottery of the year.

The man was overjoyed. He bought the ticket and put it in his pocket. From the undertaker's he went straight to the butcher shop, bought half a pig, and had it delivered to his house. He marinated the pork himself, put it on the grill, and asked his wife to cook some potatoes and other vegetables.

That night of December 21st, the official beginning of Summer, Abelardo invited his neighbors to dinner. He was in a celebratory mood. He and his wife carried the dining room table through the window and set it on the patio. Then he brought several bottles of the best grappa up from the cellar, along with links of homemade sausage.

They ate and drank, and the meat tasted more tender and juicier than ever. During dessert, Abelardo took down his accordion from the wall and began to play. Nobody knew why he looked so happy; nor did anyone think to question him. They just followed his joyful mood, drinking and singing. When the grappa ran out, the red wine began to flow, a cheaper one, and the hours became more and more festive with the celebrants singing, rocking in unison from right to left, and left to right, forming a single body of semi-drunken companions:

> *Drink this glass, this glass of wine*
> *You already drank it, you already drank it,*
> *and now it's the neighbor's turn.*

Finally, the guests thanked the saddler and his wife for their hospitality and went home, because the next day, Thursday, was a working day. It was then that Abelardo staggered to a small shed where he kept his tools and arranged them on the concrete patio, in a row as straight as his alcohol-soaked brain would allow. The embers still burning on the grill were reflected in his pupils, alight with excitement and drink. He took an iron rod, inserted it into a ring embedded in the septic tank's round cement cover, and with a forceful movement that almost made him fall backwards, lifted the lid.

Immediately the emanations of the cesspool, also called "blind pool" in that region, rose up to his nostrils as he threw, one by one and with fierce joy, all his work tools: the hammers, the knives, the sharpened steel, the awl, the punch, the riveters, the boxes of nails. Then he returned the lid to its place, wiped his hands on his pants, and went inside the house.

His wife recounted that later that night Abelardo "wanted war" and affectionately dragged her to the bedroom, where— I presume — he murmured in her ear who knows what immodest intimacies that got tangled up on his tongue. As soon as he undressed and wanted to lunge, he fell asleep on top of his wife.

Early the next morning, with a huge hangover, Abelardo grabbed the radio that was on his nightstand and tuned it to the station that was scheduled to broadcast the winning numbers of *La Gorda*. He was biting his nails. At last, the triumphant, winning figure was enunciated digit by digit. He wrote them down on a piece of paper, one by one—with unexpected lucidity but a trembling hand.

It was nowhere near his number, down to the last two digits.

"Not even the last number!" his wife would tell her neighbors later, hysterically, when referring to that morning.

When reality cleared the clouds from his brain, Abelard let out a savage howl. His wife ran to his side and found him sitting on the bed, naked and crying like a baby, with his head on top of the radio.

The episode was retold time after time amid laughter in the cafe, at the club, at family gatherings and around the soccer field. On the afternoon before the drawing on that peculiar day, Tonino had been counting the flies he was hunting, his mother reported. And he was about to reach the perfect numeral, the number nine thousand—which for him contained a supreme meaning bordering on the sacred—when Abelardo questioned him. Naturally, the Fool gave voice to the figure that hovered on his lips.

He had caught fly number eight thousand nine hundred and ninety-nine since the day he had started the count in early spring.

As for the tools of the unfortunate Abelardo, they remained in the depths of the septic tank. Not for nothing is it also called the sump, a word with the same origin as swamp, which denotes immersion, descent, sinking, disappearance. As in a cosmic black cesspool, what enters there remains submerged forever.

I would like to believe that the people took pity and pitched in to re-equip Abelardo's workshop. After all, a town like ours that appreciates horses and good saddles always needs a good saddler.

The Turks

We had moved to the city three years before. One evening, we were glued to the black-and-white screen and its coverage of John Kennedy's assassination, when Uncle Redente barged into the room. He worked in the mail car on the train that ran through Maria Susana and was in the habit of passing on gossip from there. But that day he was the bearer of some serious news that left us shaken.

"They've killed the Turk!" he burst out.

"Which one?" my mother asked, her hand on her chest.

It was a reasonable question because several individuals in town were known by the same moniker. None were Turks, by the way, but Arabs from Syria or Lebanon. Among those I remembered, there was the very Catholic Turk who owned a clothing store in front of the church. Because of his experience in liturgical matters, and his renowned piety, the parish priest had put him in charge of organizing processions, teaching catechism, managing the supply of wine in the sacristy, and other parish duties. He was a person of impeccable behavior, so the nickname "Turk" was rarely applied to him. Instead, he was generally known as Don Salman. On church holidays, the good man would be out in the street throwing his hat into the air and shouting, "Long live Our Lady!" or "Long live God!" I remember this confused me a little. As a child, I assumed that both were eternal beings and beyond the bounds of life and death. But let whoever is free from the sin of excessiveness throw the first stone!

The other pseudo-Turk owned a haberdashery and sold fabrics and items for sewing and other crafts.

I had also heard of a third, named Amir, though I had never met him and had no idea where he lived or what he did for a living.

But it's Turk number two I want to talk about, because he has a special place in my memory, thanks to an incident that set off the first spark of social conscience in me, a sense of compassion for the less unfortunate that until that moment I had reserved only for sparrows fallen out their nests on stormy nights.

They say this man opened his first business on the corner in front of the pharmacy. But I met him somewhere else, somewhere closer to my house, between the police station and the shoemaker Colina. I remember it as a place that was poorly lit and cold but had an inviting smell: a mixture of soap, coffee with cardamom, and humidity. I had no idea how many people would know the man's real name because—with that enthusiasm of ours, brought over from the motherland, for naming people after their flaws; just think of *Pepe Botella* (Joe Bottle, for Joseph Bonaparte) or *Juana La Loca* (Joanne the Mad, for a Castilian queen) to name a few—we called this man, at least behind his back, "Dirty Turk." And, as everyone knows, once one person gets a taste for the disgraceful pleasure of inventing an offensive nickname, it soon spreads like wildfire and becomes part of the communal lexicon.

Back then, his nickname meant nothing to me. What's more, it sounded like *"Deriturc,"* a single word with no adjective attached. That's how it was until the fateful day my mother sent me to the haberdashery to buy a needle.

I politely positioned myself in front of the counter and said, "Mr. Dirty Turk, I want a needle with a large eye, for wool, my mom says." And I gave him my biggest smile.

For a second, the man looked at me as if he were about to die and knew for certain he would never get to a Turkish heaven. I saw a weird flash like burning coal in his eyes as they bored into mine. He immediately dug around in his drawers, handed me the needle, and then stared at the damp walls of his shop, to absorb the affront, I guess, or maybe to suppress a desire to slap me. I handed over the money. When he gave me the change, I didn't know if his eyes were shining because they reflected the moisture on the wall, or if something had cracked inside him and his soul was slipping away. But I do know I experienced a terrible flash of recognition. I said *dirty*! Dirty Turk!

The transition to maturity is usually a slow and gradual process. But the proverbial loss of innocence is sudden. And that's how it was for me—as though I had fallen off a horse in mid-gallop. And the bitter taste in my mouth wasn't due only to my grasping my childish mistake. An entire community was at fault, and I had absorbed and naively articulated the insult.

I called him a dirty Turk!

I imagined his mouth filling with bile. I left, my cheeks red with embarrassment and rage. I had the needle in my hand, but it might as well have been a dagger piercing my heart.

This incident took place seven years before the day my uncle announced the murder, and I had remembered nothing at all about it. As a teenager, I spent my mental energy on more pressing matters (even more so than the murder of JFK), such as choosing which side to part my hair on or which comb to use for teasing it. Nonetheless, at the mention of "Turk," scattered impressions floating at the back of my mind, came to land and took shape. I knew then that the event in my childhood had always crouched inside me, silently pointing at me with an accusing finger.

"Which one of the Turks was it?" my mother asked again.

I silently prayed it was not the one with the needle. I hoped the victim was a different Turk, someone I did not know, because the one I did know had already carried his cross, or whatever it is a Muslim carries, in the form of the shameful nickname people had tormented him with. I also remembered that, after that long-ago afternoon involving the needle, I had imagined myself in a moment of sudden courage taking back my mistake and stanching the wound. I saw myself going up to him and explaining in a quiet whisper that I had not meant to cause offence, that it was because other people, people who weren't bad, just silly, thoughtlessly repeated what they'd heard... But I never found the courage or maturity to do it. And so I hauled my guilt away and put off apologizing until I forgot about it. And now it could be too late. I prayed the heavens would forgive my negligence.

Years later I was able to put a name to the racist abuse that went hand in hand with ignorance: *Turkophobia*. Little did we know about the suffering in the countries of the Middle East under the Ottoman Empire, where the immigrants we met came from: Syria, Lebanon, Jordan, Armenia, Palestine ... all regions where Arabic was spoken, or the Ladino of the Sephardic Jews, or another language not closely related to Turkish, the official language.

Nor did we know that before World War I and

the defeat of the Ottomans, and specifically during reign of the despot Sultan Abdul Hamid's (known as the "Red Sultan" because of the blood spilled in his name), the provinces of the empire were a battlefield. Even the words "freedom" "democracy," "rights," and the like had been banned and banished from the dictionary. The practice of exclusion became so entrenched that even in the second decade of the twenty first century, a hundred years later, phrases such as "climate change," "emissions reduction," or "Paris Agreement" were redacted from the reports issued by the US Department of Energy.

In those days, the wealthy people of countries under Turkish rule migrated to Europe, escaping both the sultanate's tyranny and religious struggles. The poor opted for Latin America. They all arrived on these shores at the beginning of the twentieth century with the same document in hand: a Turkish passport. Which explains the generic and deceptive nickname.

The Islamophobia prevailing in certain media impelled me to revisit the event of my past. But six decades of remembering and forgetting are no small thing, and I found more questions than answers. I do not intend to recount my ersatz Turk's life history but to offer scraps of stories about him that I have stitched together from various sources.

You may say that the life of a man whose name we don't even know is not especially significant. But whose life is? We are no less perishable than butterflies that live only for a day, no more persistent than an outbreath that evaporates as soon as we utter a single word. Here, then, is what I know of Dirty Turk, whom I will now call DT, to avoid any associations brought about by the nickname that so upset me and, of course, out of respect for his solitary existence.

He must have been around sixty years old the day I went to the haberdashery. Slight in stature and ashen faced, he seemed to be wasting away. He was a man of few words, serious and measured. I wonder in what corner of the past he had forgotten his sense of joyfulness. I never knew if his aloofness hid shyness, sadness, or disdain. My friends would go to buy a spool of thread from him just to hear him quote the price—"*un beso, dos besos*" ("a kiss, two kisses") instead of "*un peso, dos pesos.*" They left his shop creased with laughter. The *pe* was always too explosive for his tongue. But I also sensed that a curtain of misunderstanding came between him and his mostly adult customers.

Because of how reserved he was, little or nothing was known about his life before he arrived in the village, let alone before immigrating to the country. However, he was a little more forthcoming with Don Salman, perhaps because they both could speak colloquial Arabic, their native language, and laugh over the small differences in everyday expressions. DT once opened up and told Don Salman his story. They say it happened because he was flushed from a glass of strong Cabrini communion wine that the shopkeeper brought out from the sacristy to serve his friend (and replaced the next day, I am assured). I suppose DT must have thrown away the list of libations banned by his religion. And since Salman was a confidant of a distant relative of mine with whom he would stand outside the church, handing out pictures of Our Lady from a silver platter, luckily this story has not been lost. I'm not saying the woman was a gossip. She simply saw no reason to keep the story to herself, especially as there wasn't much to do besides attending church, drinking mate, and talking.

When I collected these stories, I understood why DT found no pleasure in talking about his past.

It appears that he was born in Syria around 1893. Life in his homeland was difficult enough, but his family managed through work and prayer. The days were long and spent doubled over hand looms, spinning and weaving for a fellow who worked in the cotton industry. The nights were short and populated by ghouls, the well-known creatures from *The Thousand and One Nights* that roam the dark. Winters were harsh. Snow covered the orchards and the animals died from cold. In summer, they were lashed both by the extreme heat and a yellow wind that brought cholera (so called because of the "choleric" nature of the disease, my source explained).

As a teenager, DT became addicted to breeding pigeons, a common hobby—or vice, they said– among males in those parts. It drained him of the little money he made and created major problems with his family. He also had another pastime: he joined a gang of young Muslims like him, who threw stones at Christians on the other side of the canal that divided the city by faith; the Christians in turn hurled them back with equal ferocity.

He soon realized that religious enemies might be on the other side, but the danger on his was more of a threat, because the empire's spies, who everyone feared, lurked on his home patch. The members of the underground movement DT was a part of would gather at the mill to discuss their strategy of resistance. One day, they were found out and the Red Sultan's forces slashed their way in with their sabers to break up the meeting and put a stop to any attempt at revolt against the regime. DT witnessed the massacre from behind some bags of flour and saw many of his colleagues killed. I can't help but wonder today if this sowed the seeds of his somber disposition.

He knew that night he had to flee. He left the mill, now strewn with corpses, and arrived home broken hearted to say goodbye to his family. Then he mounted the best horse they had and, under cover of darkness, sped away at full gallop. Some days later he arrived at the port of Beirut, where he found an emigration agent who, for a small price (plus the horse), put him on a boat to Alexandria, then one to Genoa, and finally one to Buenos Aires. The latter was a coaster, one of those vessels that docked at numerous ports and took two months to get there.

He had chosen that particular Latin American city because he had an uncle there called Mamet.

Mamet had been both a dentist and a hairdresser in Syria, since the two professions went hand in hand in that country at the time. One day, an outraged patient-client, who had had the wrong tooth pulled, set the combination dentist office and barbershop on fire—and consequently the uncle lost his most precious piece of furniture: his chair. A resentful Mamet set off on an immigrant ship, arrived in Buenos Aires, and began to thrive there, not as a dentist this time but as a barber.

DT knew his uncle would welcome him.

He was in his twenties when he arrived in Argentina, undernourished, weak, and a nervous wreck. After a few weeks at his uncle's house he recovered, but it wasn't long before he had another setback. In this New World city, he saw women walking around with their arms uncovered and patting men on the back in public without provoking their husbands' wrath. Cultural shock together with the pain of being uprooted plunged him back into a dark mental state that bordered on delirium.

But, as the saying goes, nothing bad lasts for a hundred years and no one would put up with it for as long as that, DT overcame this too and rebuilt his life thanks to the money Mamet lent him for a small investment. With his rudimentary Spanish, DT went from door to door throughout the barrios of Buenos Aires, selling fabrics, perfumes, soaps and other items he had acquired wholesale, and charging for them in monthly installments. And so began his career as a businessman.

There's a gap in this story because no one knows how or when he came to our village. They say that it was around 1940 and that he set up his business on a corner in front of the pharmacy. The only trace of his dovecote back in Syria was a painting of a dove on the wall of his shop; of his earlier militancy, just a bitter memory.

It was from other sources that I became aware of DT's third nervous breakdown, this time due to finances. The corner haberdashery did not do enough business to cover the rent, and he had to move to another, much smaller place. Perhaps the depression that some men often fall into when they reach forty or fifty took him back to his past. Maybe an ill wind suddenly blew open a window and a gust of pain swept through his heart. He gave into sad memories, and lice, and gradually broke ties with reality. Cobwebs filled the corners of the little shop, and cockroaches lay scattered across the floor. Customers only patronized the shop when they wanted to be served quickly; almost no one ventured in because the shopkeeper there was definitely a dirty Turk. More taciturn than ever, the man existed in limbo between sanity and madness.

Whether it was the strong Cabrini wine from the sacristy that Don Salman sometimes treated him to or the sound of Arabic, DT regained his senses as he had on other occasions. He dusted off the cobwebs, swept the floor, scrubbed his nails, cut his hair, got rid of the lice and restocked his supplies with needles and all kinds of thread. He took charge, inside and out. But Dirty's unkind epithet remained, like the permanent scars on the faces of those who have recovered from chickenpox.

DT kept his political militancy to himself for decades. Even after the Turkish empire fell, and Syria became part of the French protectorate and then finally acquired independence, this Syrian, who lived in the far reaches of the world, still feared reprisals from some former Ottoman spy.

My uncle unclipped the clothespins from his

trousers legs, which I think he used to keep his cuffs from getting caught in his bike chains.

"Did they kill D-- ... the Turk from the haber-dashery?" I asked him.

"They told me it was Amir Ali, the Turk from the other barrio," he replied. "He was struck on the head with an iron bar. By the time Dr. Traslucero arrived, he was already dead."

"How horrible!" my mother exclaimed, lowering the volume on the television. "Do you know who did it?"

"They're investigating."

Well, at least it wasn't the Turk with the needle, I thought. Maybe I should write him a letter of apology, even though the timing was off. But better late than never, I said to myself, during one of those ethical-philosophical flaps I occasionally got myself into. A few days earlier I had read, as part of my homework, a saying attributed to Socrates: "It is better to suffer an injustice than to commit one." The phrase had made a strong impression on me. But it was no easy matter to send the letter. I had neither the recipient's name nor his address. And I wasn't going to write "Mr. Dirty Turk, Main Street, between the shoemaker and the precinct" on the letter either. It would be a needless, absurd mistake. I asked my father, without disclosing why, if he knew his name. He said no. I didn't pursue it further.

So much for my good intentions, which lasted for as long as the glow of a lightning bug.

As far as the murder of this Amir went, policeman Godofredo charged a Hilares and a Corrales, my uncle later told me. They were seen leaving Amir's business at night with a bag that could well have contained stolen money. They raided the house they were hiding out in and found the bag with no money in it, just bloody clothes. The two were taken off to jail and beaten, along with some other suspects, all boys from the *barrio*. Hilares's mother made a stink. She ran through her *barrio* and ours too, screaming at the top of her lungs, brandishing her son's work clothes, and clamoring for justice.

"It's cow's blood, for God's sake!" the woman screamed.

Everyone knew the workers at the municipal slaughterhouse left work covered in filth. Godofredo had to release the defendants, stained as they were with innocent bovine blood.

It was also speculated that it could have been the "Hungarians" who had arrived by truck a few days before. But that was misleading guesswork, and no one was convinced. Those gypsies, who were neither from Egypt nor Hungary but from Romania, certainly had a reputation as thieves and kidnappers, but they were not murderers. It wasn't the first time they had camped on the outskirts of town, scattering their colorful clothes over the green alfalfa, and there had never been that kind of crime associated with them.

It was later rumored that a nephew might have killed him to steal the money he had hidden under the mattress. But there was no evidence.

During the weeks I've worked on remembering and looking into this event, I've taken comfort in knowing that at least DT did not meet a violent death. But a few days ago, my confidence was dashed during a lively online conversation with a group of childhood friends. Having listened to my pleas for help, they agreed to collaborate on my project by going over what they remembered about DT.

"Didn't the Turk from downtown close down his haberdashery and move to a farm in the barrio ... and didn't they begin calling him the "Turk of Dogs"?

"I thought Dirty Turk was the one Dr. Traslucero's daughter described as having been found dead in the neighborhood on August 21, 1963. His name was Don Amin."

"That name and date both match what I found in the cemetery and sent to Rita. His name was Anin."

"So Don Amin or Anin and Dirty Turk were one and the same?" I cut in, furious at having my version of the story ruined, not to mention the grief I felt over the evil end that had befallen *my* Turk.

"I believe the one with the dogs moved to the big house in front of the square."

"I didn't even know they'd killed Dirty Turk or that he'd moved into the barrio. When he died, some nephews came to sell off his things on the street where the police station is, not in front of the square."

"Aren't you thinking of the nephew they say killed Don Amir?"

"Who's Amir?"

Memory is a prism of opaque and deceptive crystals. Inside the mind there's a judicious gardener who prunes memories that are unnecessary and frees up space for new information. Without this clearing out, our fate would be as sad as that of Funes the

Memorious whose mind was so cluttered with detail he was unable to think in abstract terms. But there's no one like Borges's Funes in my village. That's why the facts and names of the past now at my disposal overlap and reassemble themselves like the pieces of color in a kaleidoscope.

Never mind. Recreating characters and events from the past have some magic to it. So I'll settle for magic and for having resurrected Dirty Turk's memory—regardless of whether his name was Amin or Amir—in a gesture of posthumous apology.

Amalia and I

First from left, seated, my mother, *señora* Elvira Belletti de
Sturam, music and folkloric dance teacher.

The Cure

Mr. Ripoll, wine seller.

Dissonances I

La Virgen volviendo de la procesión en el patio de la antigua iglesia

The Virgen Mary returning to church in procession enters
the church yard.

Dissonances II

One of several diagonal streets in María Susana

The Turks

DT beside his store scale

Author's acknowledgment

To the friends of my beloved hometown, María Susana, for helping me unearth memories that gave rise to the original version of this book, *Los huesitos de mamá y otros relatos.*

Special thanks to editor Stephanie Lawyer and writer Joyce Yarrow for their invaluable help with my English translation. To my daughters Karen, Clarice, and Elisa Wirkala, for their wise suggestions, and to my husband, Elwin Wirkala, who for the past forty-eight years has listened to my childhood stories and encouraged me to write them down.

Made in the USA
Middletown, DE
17 July 2022